Edge of the Abyss

By

Robert Fisher

Edge of the Abyss – Shadow World Book II
Copyright © 2019 Robert Fisher
ISBN: 978-1-970153-10-1
Library of Congress Control Number: 2019916263

La Maison Publishing, Inc.
Vero Beach, Florida
The Hibiscus City
lamaisonpublishing@gmail.com

Chapter 1

The Past is but Prologue

It had been three months since the Belarusian Civil War ended via a peace treaty mediated by the United Nations. Now that the war had ended it was time to deal with the destruction and suffering that the conflict had left in its wake. Almost immediately following the cessation of hostilities the UN, EU, and Red Cross – along with several other countries and relief organizations – began dispatching teams to provide aid to the populace of the ravaged nation. Relief camps and hospitals had been set up across the country with many located in some of the most battle-scarred areas. All of them were guarded by UN soldiers, most of whom were either American or European. At the moment, a Lockheed AC-130 belonging to the Red Cross was en route to the capital city of Minsk delivering supplies and relief.

The plane had once belonged to the United States Air Force, used as a gunship. Eventually it was sold to the Red Cross and converted into a cargo plane. The irony of a warplane on a mission of peace was not lost on the plane's seven passengers. Some of them had even joked about it. However, one of them in particular saw nothing humorous about it. To Mai Yunao, the tools of war repulsed her not only morally but also personally.

Mai was a young and attractive Chinese woman in her mid-twenties; today she wore a white t-shirt with blue jeans. Despite having traveled across the world as a relief worker, she couldn't stand the long boring flights. She brought magazines with her to read, *Time* and *Entertainment Weekly*, both of which she had read twice since boarding the plane in London. She sighed as she adjusted her glasses, picking up the copy of *Time* yet again to study the cover. A photographer had captured a haunting photo of a child looking over the ruins of what was once his home.

Only war can cause this kind of destruction and human suffering. Even the fury of Mother Nature is nothing compared to man's inhumanity to man, thought Mai. *I will never get used to seeing the pain left in war's wake ... but that's probably a good thing. At least it proves I still have a conscience.*

She put the magazine down, deciding to listen to the conversation of the two men sitting across from her instead, relief workers from the Red Cross's London office. Three Hispanic men sat together at the end of the plane; she wasn't sure what their role was here. Medics? Maintenance? Their clothing gave no clues.

Mai closed her eyes and leaned back to listen unobtrusively. The relief workers were talking about a mysterious explosion that had destroyed a Belarusian military bunker three months earlier. It was quite the topic of conversation. Fodder for conspiracy theorists the world over.

Leave it to the inspectors and politicians to obsess over such things. While my team and I focus on the more important matter of helping those who have been displaced and injured in the conflict, she thought as she listened.

Despite her relative lack of interest in the subject, she couldn't help but have some curiosity about it. As the men had nothing new to share, however, she dismissed them mentally, choosing to focus on what to do when the plane arrived in Minsk. As if on cue, the co-pilot stepped out of the cockpit, a young American with a thick Minnesota accent which reminded Mai of the movie *Fargo.*

"We're almost there; everyone buckle up!" he yelled.

Something in the co-pilot's expression made Mai turn around in her seat in time to see the three men at the other end of the plane look at each other, nod, and reach into their bags to pull out handguns. Mai had seen enough guns in her life to recognize them as M9 Berettas. She watched in horror as one of the men aimed his gun at the co-pilot and shot him in the head before running past the body to the cockpit.

The other two grabbed the two terrified relief workers and moved them to the end of the plane. Mai was terrified too, but she forced herself not to show it. She knew men like these fed on the fear they instilled in their victims.

Mai had always thought that her father's profession would result in something like this. She stood and held up her hands in surrender. "Don't hurt them; it's me you want!" yelled Mai.

The men ignored her as they barked orders in Portuguese to the two terrified workers. To them, apparently, she posed no threat. She sat back down, observing everything.

Mai would not have put it past her father to send men to "rescue" her if he thought she was in danger. However the men he would sent would only kill civilians if necessary. *What is going on?* Thought Mai as she tried to stay calm.

Just then a gunshot rang out from the cockpit; the gunman who had run into cockpit emerged, yelling to the other two before returning. At that point the leader – Mai assumed he was the leader, anyway, based on his demeanor – yelled something back to his comrades in Portuguese. *The first gunman must be piloting the plane*, Mai thought, but the impact of that fact paled in comparison to her concern for the relief workers being held at the back.

Suddenly the cargo door at the rear of the plane opened with a loud mechanical yawn as wind filled the plane. Mai looked on in horror as the gunmen dragged the two workers to the end of the plane. It was clear what was about to happen; she couldn't be silent anymore.

Mai stood up and yelled at the gunmen, begging them to stop. Even if they could hear her over the roar of the wind and the pleading of the workers, they ignored her again, tossing the terrified workers out of the plane.

Once the men had disappeared out the opening, the gunmen closed the door and shifted their attention to Mai.

"Why?!" Mai yelled.

Upon hearing the insulting challenge of a mere woman, the man she believed to be the leader walked up to her and hit her in the face with the back of his hand. Mai fell to the floor and cradled her cheek in pain.

"Watch your tongue, woman! Or you will lose it," he said in English with a thick Brazilian accent.

The other gunmen picked her up and handcuffed her to the seat. The leader then knelt down on one knee in front of her and gently lifted up her head.

"Such a pretty face. 'A shame you won't live long enough for anyone to appreciate it," he said.

"Just tell me why they had to die," said Mai through tears. "They did nothing!"

The man stood up and smiled slyly. "They aren't the first innocents to die because of your father's sins."

*****

Simultaneously across the world in seven different countries, the whole affair was watched on computer screens via satellite by a group of eight powerful men called the Board of Directors, the leaders of the enigmatic organization known as the Networc. Each of them had a codename since their true identities were secret, even to one another.

Only their leader, Mr. Zero, knew their identities.

"Well, gentlemen, I'd say that went well," said Mr. Zero. The computer blurred their faces and scrambled their voices.

"Yes, let's hope the Cartel fulfills its part of the deal," Mr. Three replied.

"I'm more concerned about that Silhouette agent. He could still pose a threat to us," said Mr. Six.

"Simon Kane?" Mr. Zero asked with a roll of his eyes.

"Yes, Simon and his team were responsible for the failure of Project: Big Picture," added the newest director. Mr. Four had joined the Board after his predecessor's termination three months earlier.

"True, but he's just one man chasing ghosts. Right now the situation on Sankan is more important ... and besides, who gives a damn about Simon Kane?" Mr. Zero replied.

Chapter 2

Veteran of the Psychic Wars

This was not Simon Kane's first time in Bangkok, but as he walked through the park he couldn't help but wonder if it would be his last. Ever since he quit Silhouette and left the United States three months earlier, he had been branded an enemy of the state.

He knew, all too well, that if a retired Silhouette agent left the United States, they were immediately re-classified, tracked down, and killed on sight by Silhouette's elite internal affairs agency, codenamed Blacklist Protocol. Simon had been ready and waiting for one of them to show up. To his surprise, in the three months he had been in Thailand, there had been no sign of Blacklist. It was baffling; due to Silhouette's status as an off-the-books black ops branch of the CIA, rogue agents were *always* dealt with immediately ... with a bullet.

But now? Nothing. Simon wondered what was going on at Langley in general, and specifically, why they hadn't tried to kill him yet. What really irritated him, though, was that he couldn't find a hint of the Networc or the agent Stanislaw. After looking all over Thailand and its capital, he had found nothing. Occasionally, he thought about leaving, despite having no leads and nowhere to go.

No amount of time or trouble would stop him from making the Networc pay for the death of the only woman he ever loved, his ex-wife and fellow Silhouette agent Sheila Goodbody. When he closed his eyes he could still see her being shot right in front of him by the Networc's mysterious agent, Counselor Black, on that mission in Belarus. He had witnessed many deaths during his career, but hers was the only one that haunted him.

As Simon walked, he reminisced; the five years he and Sheila were married were the best years of his life. *All good things must end*, he thought bitterly. Shortly after they were discharged from the agency, Simon's alcoholism had resulted in their divorce. He ultimately conquered the addiction and had remained sober since. When both Simon and Sheila were reenlisted by Silhouette three months ago, they had fallen back in love.

Simon always looked forward to the end of a mission, but especially so with that one. After all the time apart they would finally be able to live a comfortable life together. His hopes were shattered by a single bullet that fueled his thirst for revenge. His singular quest for vengeance led him to Bangkok, but that wasn't what brought him to this small park today.

As he sat down on a park bench he turned his attention from the past and focused instead on his present surroundings. The day was warm and sunny; the park was full of people enjoying their Saturday afternoon. Simon Kane, however, was not there for enjoyment or relaxation. Three days ago

Simon had received a call. Someone wanted to meet him at this particular bench at two-thirty on Saturday, but Simon had no idea who the person was; the voice was scrambled. Simon didn't know exactly what made him take the call seriously.

It could be a trap, for all I know, he thought.

Just in case it was, Simon had his pistol with him, a Jericho 941. It was in a shoulder holster concealed under his dark blue trench coat. Simon was tall with a muscular frame, permanently tan due to his mother's Italian heritage. His short black hair was slicked backward, framing a rough yet handsome face despite the black eye patch covering what remained of his right eye.

Simon checked his watch: three o'clock. His mystery caller, whoever he or she was, was late. Simon shrugged and decided to wait another fifteen minutes before leaving. He looked around the park, taking in the woman with a baby stroller who was just entering the enclosure. An old man sat on the bench across from him reading a newspaper. As paranoid as it would sound to anyone else, he knew that anyone there could be an assassin from Blacklist Protocol.

The good news is that I can see the entrance to the park from here. And my pistol's fully loaded, thought Simon.

An attractive female jogger ran past as Simon subtly watched her with his one good eye.

"Nice day, isn't it, MONOLITH?" said a familiar voice in a British accent behind him.

Simon turned around slowly, surprised to hear his codename again, his hand instinctively jumping to the Jericho 941 in his shoulder holster.

"Yes, it is, SABRE," Simon replied. Recognizing the face that went with the voice, he let go of the pistol.

SABRE's real name was Nigel Solo. He was an agent of Equinox, a black ops division of MI6, England's answer to Silhouette. Simon had worked with him in the past on joint missions; he was a good man and one of the few people in the world that Simon trusted.

"How gratifying it is to be remembered, Simon," said Nigel.

His accent always reminded Simon of one of the actors that played James Bond, but he could never remember which one. "A little far from home, aren't you, Nigel?" Simon asked sarcastically.

Solo grinned as he sat down next to Simon. Nigel was handsome, with the pale complexion common to Englishmen coupled with the stereotypical smooth, controlled demeanor of British spies, both real and imaginary. He wore a gray blazer over a white dress shirt, black tie and gray pants. Comparatively, Simon wore a black button-down, green cargo pants, and his dark blue trench coat. Overdressed to conceal weaponry, neither of them was bothered by the heat due to their special forces training.

Nigel fingered Simon's coat sleeve. "You still wear that bloody thing?" joked Nigel.

"What can I say – I'm consistent," replied Simon dryly. He crossed his arms so he could grab his pistol quickly. Just in case.

Nigel knew what Simon was thinking. He'd be thinking the same thing, if their roles were reversed.

"So … what are you doing here, Nigel?" asked Simon.

"First of all, relax; I'm here neither to kill you nor to bring you in," Nigel answered. "My superiors have bigger problems to deal with than you."

"Of course you do," said Simon as he pulled a toothpick out of his pocket and stuck it between his teeth.

"We are curious about your intentions in this region, however," Nigel continued.

"And why does London care about little old me?" asked Simon with a smirk.

"We have several …. interests … in this part of the world. We want to know your intentions, to see if they pose a threat to us," Nigel explained. "They sent me to find out since we have worked together in the past."

Same old tradecraft, thought Simon with a shrug. *Still, that can't be the only reason London sent him all the way here.* "Tell your people not to worry. I'm here tracking down the Networc," he answered.

"I see. And what if Her Majesty's interests stand between you and the Networc?" Nigel asked.

Simon looked his old friend directly in the eye. "Then things will get ... interesting," he answered.

"Not *too* interesting, I hope," said Nigel.

The men were quiet for a few minutes. Equinox agents were every bit as efficient and highly trained as their American counterparts in Silhouette. *If things do get "interesting," would Equinox send Nigel to kill me at some point?* Simon pondered.

"Simon," said Nigel. His tone was now that of a friend, not a fellow spy. "I'm sorry about Sheila," he said softly. "She was one of the best."

At the mention of her name, Simon's mind again flashed back to the control room in the Belarusian weapons lab where Sheila was killed. "Thanks," he said quietly.

"Simon, why are you doing this? Black is dead," Nigel asked quizzically.

The mournful look in Simon's eye was suddenly replaced by the laser focus that he was known for. "His bosses are still out there. His organization is still out there. They're just as guilty as Black," said Simon sternly.

Nigel could tell he meant every word of what he said; he had made a similar vow himself, years ago. "Simon, I believe it was Confucius who said: before you embark on a journey of revenge, dig two graves," he said calmly.

"Don't give me that shit, Nigel! By that logic you should forgive the Devil Woman for what she did to you and your team!" growled Simon.

Nigel looked insulted and offended. Simon instantly regretted his outburst; he knew the Devil Woman was a sore spot for Nigel.

"I'm sorry. My emotions got the better of me," Simon capitulated.

Nigel shook his head. "It's fine. That bitch is dead and gone," he said. "Still, I understand how you feel – but you can't do it alone."

Simon hated to admit it, but Nigel was right. In the three months since embarking on this path of vengeance, he had discovered nothing about the Networc, not to mention that if he *could* find them, he'd need help. He knew all too well how ruthless the Networc's forces were.

"Fine, then. What's your suggestion?" asked Simon.

"Simple. Defect to Equinox and we'll help you," Nigel answered.

There it is – the real reason he's here, realized Simon.

It's not like Simon hadn't considered defecting. Equinox, being a division of MI6, would be able to accomplish more than Simon could on his own. In the process, though, he would most likely have to hand over every shred of intel he knew about Silhouette. That would be committing treason, the very reason why it was deemed a capital offense for retired Silhouette agents to leave the country. Still, despite everything, Simon was no traitor. Besides, the Networc made this personal. He wanted to do it on his own, without the shackles of the espiocracy.

"Tempting offer, Nigel, but the answer's no. Besides, you know I hate British food," answered Simon.

"I see. Well then, I have a question for you: What will you do once you've gotten your revenge?" inquired Nigel.

It was a fair question, one that Simon had asked himself many times since leaving his homeland. "I'll figure that out when I get there," Simon replied dismissively.

"Nigel, these people ... they're different. They're well- funded and highly trained. Not to mention the fact that Silhouette had no data on them. And we both know London knows nothing, either," continued Simon.

Nigel shrugged in answer. He couldn't say anything, but he knew Simon was right. "Well, in that case, good luck – and if there's anything you need, just let me know," he said with a sigh as he stood up.

Simon stood too, and they shook hands. "That offer is always on the table. Just so you know," said Nigel.

"I'll keep that in mind. See you on the far side," said Simon as Nigel turned to leave.

"Not too soon, I hope, replied Nigel slyly. "Oh, and by the way – you should give fish and chips another shot."

"Not a chance in hell," Simon replied with a rakish grin.

Nigel laughed as he walked out of the park toward his car. Simon waited until he was gone before leaving himself, walking back to the hotel room he had been living in. As Simon wove in and out around Bangkok's sidewalk throngs, he couldn't help but wonder what was happening at Silhouette's headquarters in Langley, Virginia at that very minute. His meeting with Nigel was the first real contact that he had had with anyone in the intelligence community since he left America. The real question, the one he had been asking over and over again while a reasonable answer eluded him was as simple as it was bleak: Why, after three months of his being a rogue agent, hadn't Silhouette tried to kill him?

More vexing, though, was the Networc. In three long months, he may have come a long way geographically, but he was no closer to his goal. Where were they? *Who* were they?

Chapter 3

Off the Books

General Mark Connors was not having a good day and he knew it was only going to get worse. In addition to having been stuck in traffic on the way to the George Bush Center for Intelligence – headquarters for both the CIA and Silhouette in Langley, Virginia – he had a meeting at five o'clock this afternoon with the Director of the CIA, David Campbell.

Connors, the leader of Silhouette, answered directly to the President – a fact that irked a bureaucrat like Campbell. Not only was Campbell a micromanager, the man harbored a great dislike of Connors and what Campbell regarded as the general's unorthodox methods. This was fine with

Connors. The feeling was mutual – which only added to the sense of impending drama.

Connors despised being micromanaged, considering it an impediment to Silhouette's effectiveness. Connors leaned back in his office chair, rubbing his eyes from the strain of reading a rather lengthy report from an agent they'd sent to infiltrate and sabotage an Iranian nuclear enrichment facility. Connors placed the report on his desk and checked his watch. Five-thirty. He smiled slightly, knowing that David was probably sitting in his office stewing in his own agitation. *The man does love his schedules,* he thought.

Connors stood, straightened his tie, and walked out of his office to the elevator down the hall. Once inside, he pushed the button for the top floor and watched the doors close in front of him. When the elevator doors opened again, he exited, walked down another hallway, made a left at the end and walked through a door marked: DIRECTOR OF CENTRAL INTELLIGENCE AGENCY.

Campbell's secretary, Kathleen, sat at her desk typing on her computer's keyboard. She looked up as he came through the door, greeting him with a little nod.

"Hello, Kathleen. How's Dave?" asked Connors.

"Pissed," Kathleen grunted apathetically.

"When isn't he?" Connors replied dryly.

Kathleen grinned. "I miss Gina," she muttered. Kathleen had been with the agency long enough to remember several other leaders, all of whom she liked more than Campbell.

"So do I. And we know who to thank for firing her," replied Campbell.

"Kathleen! Is he here yet?" yelled Campbell from his office. Connors had the distinct impression that this wasn't the first time that afternoon he had yelled the exact same words.

"Better get in there," said Kathleen dryly, gesturing toward the inner doorway with her head.

"Always a pleasure, Kathleen," said Connors with a smile before walking into Campbell's office.

Campbell sat in the swivel chair behind his desk looking like an angry high school principal. Connors could tell right away that Campbell was indeed in a bad mood, one that would likely only get worse.

Connors sat down in a chair in front of the desk, unfazed by the ornery stare Campbell gave him.

Campbell was not a man for pleasantries. "Mark, do you know why I called you here?" he inquired.

"I parked in your spot again?" asked Connors sarcastically. In reality he knew full well what this meeting was about.

"Cut the bullshit, Connors! POTUS might like you, but I don't! And I like your handling of the MONOLITH situation even less!" Campbell barked.

Connors sighed, "Which part, Dave? Because as I recall, Operation: SAVAGE GARDEN was a success," Connors said mockingly.

"Yes, yes, Operation: SAVAGE GARDEN was a success despite the one casualty, but that isn't the point," said Campbell dismissively.

"Well then, what *is* the point," Connors asked impatiently.

"You know as well as I do that any retired Silhouette agent that leaves U.S. soil is declared an enemy of the state and must be eliminated via Blacklist Protocol immediately," explained Campbell with the bored tone of a teacher repeating himself.

"However," he continued, swiveling his chair so that he wasn't looking directly at Connors, "in the last three months you have not made any effort to track down or deploy any Blacklist Protocol agents to kill Simon Kane, codename: MONOLITH."

Campbell swiveled the chair abruptly back to face Connors and sat taller for effect. "I know you have a reason for it, which you refuse to tell me! For the last time: Why. Is. He. Still. Alive?" asked Campbell, his voice increasing in volume with each word of his final question.

Connors took a deep breath to collect his thoughts. "Contrary to what you think, we *are* watching him. According to our Intel he's in Bangkok at the moment. As to why he isn't dead, it's simple: He's not our biggest problem. The Networc is," answered Connors.

Campbell rolled his eyes as he leaned back in his chair.

"As I see it, Silhouette's number one goal right *now* is to hunt down and destroy the Networc," continued Connors.

"Yet in three months you have found nothing to support that they even exist," interrupted Campbell accusingly. "And neither have the British, the French, Interpol or anyone else for that matter," he explained.

"Exactly! The Networc has not only evaded detection by every major intelligence agency on the planet for God only knows how long, but it almost succeeded in stealing several nuclear weapons from a country that they claim to have destabilized. And God only knows what *else* they've done or what they will do *next!*" Connors rebuked.

Connors paused before continuing. "You know as well as I do that despite Silhouette's incredibly high success rate, we have been unable to find these people. Ergo, if *we* can't find them, then you know it's bad," he said.

"What does this have to do with Simon? You don't know what *he's* going to do next either!" Campbell asked anxiously.

"Quite the contrary. I know *exactly* what he'll do next, which is why he's still alive," responded Connors.

"Which is what, exactly?" asked Campbell impatiently.

"He's going to hunt down and destroy the Networc for us," Connors answered, confident that he knew how Campbell would respond based on the mixture of curiosity and confusion on his face.

"Yes, it actually is that simple. I know how he thinks," continued Connors. "I commanded the man for years. Hell, I'm the one that brought him into Silhouette! In all that time I've learned how to predict what he'll do," Connors explained.

Connor's mouth was dry from all the talking, but he noticed a pitcher of water beside a small stack of plastic cups on Campbell's desk. He leaned forward, filled one of the cups and took a long drink.

"Help yourself," Campbell grunted.

Connors ignored the sarcasm as he set the cup down and resumed speaking where he'd left off, refreshed from the water. "Simon Kane is a man of intense focus and sheer will.

Essentially, he needs a mission. When these people killed his wife, they gave him a doozy," said Connors.

"He's out for revenge and knowing him, he'll get it, come hell or high water," continued Connors. "My plan is to let him hunt down and destroy the Networc, then bring him in once he's done." Finished with his explanation, he poured another cupful of water and downed it.

Campbell waited a few seconds. "What if you're wrong and he defects?" he asked.

Connors would never admit it, but it was a fair question. The whole reason Blacklist Protocol existed was to prevent Silhouette's secrets and its very existence from being revealed to the world by former or rogue agents. *Not Simon, though,* he thought.

"Simon is many things, but a traitor is not one of them. Believe me, if there is one man on the planet who can get to the Networc, it is Simon," said Connors.

Campbell pressed his fingers together, processing Connors' explanation.

Finally Campbell spoke, narrowing his eyes skeptically. "Let me get this straight.

Your plan is to let Simon hunt down and destroy the Networc for us, while keeping him under surveillance?"

"Exactly. POTUS doesn't like it either, but it's the only choice we've got to bring down the Networc," answered Connors.

"What about Sankan Island? If he goes there, we've lost him," said Campbell.

"Did you forget about Task Force 666?" asked Connors smugly.

Campbell frowned as he tried to remember, then shrugged in defeat. "Regrettably, yes I did," he said. "Remind me."

Connors grinned at the request; Task Force 666 was one of Silhouette's most successful, albeit controversial, endeavors.

"After ECHO 9 was shut down, we needed to replace it quickly. We released two high level criminals from Guantanamo Bay, recruited them, and assigned a top Silhouette agent as their handler. We sent them to Sankan Island to spy on the Triad, Syndicate and Cartel ... and do an occasional mission for us," explained Connors.

He continued as if he were a proud father speaking of his child's accomplishments. "They've been very effective. On the island they're known as the Flying Fish Trading Company doing jobs for the Triad, the Cartel and the Syndicate."

"I'm starting to remember them now. As I recall, you nicknamed them the Goon Squad, right?" asked Campbell.

"Yes," replied Connors.

"One thing, though. These criminals that were recruited, who are they, exactly?" asked Campbell.

"Fiona Ramos, codename: BARRACUDA. And Kenji Yamada, codename: SNAPPER," answered Connors.

"And their handler?" asked Campbell.

"His name is Ben Martin, codename: EYEBALL," answered Connors.

The Flying Fish Trading Company was not Silhouette's only front company. It was actually the smaller of the two dummy companies maintained by Silhouette. The larger company was the international corporation known as Twilight Industries. Twilight Industries served two important purposes: It raised the funds needed to fund Silhouette by designing and selling the same state-of-the-art electronics Silhouette agents used. As a result of this, Silhouette was financially self-sustaining; none of Silhouette's expenses appeared on the CIA's budget. Their second task was to provide Silhouette with any materials it might need to create special tools and equipment for field agents.

"What does the Goon Squad have to do with Simon Kane?" asked Campbell.

"I've instructed EYEBALL and his team to do everything they can to covertly observe – and if need be, support – Simon, should he arrive on the island," Connors answered with smug grin.

"You *what*!? Why?" asked Campbell in surprise.

"We can't have him getting kidnapped or killed if he does go there," explained Connors.

Campbell thought for a minute, letting everything Connors had said sink in.

"If you have a better plan I'd love to hear it," said Connors impatiently.

"No, no, I don't. I guess you're right. It's the best – the only – way to find them. Still, it sounds awfully risky. But good luck, all the same," said Campbell disingenuously.

"Thanks," replied Connors, feeling slightly insulted as he stood. Campbell rose as well and offered an unenthusiastic hand across the desk.

As Connors got back on the elevator, he couldn't help but wonder what Simon was doing right then in Bangkok. *Just after six here, so around five a.m. there …*

When he returned to his office, he closed the door before pulling out his cell phone and dialing the number of the Flying Fish Trading Company. His phone had special encryption software on it that automatically scrambled all calls to prevent anyone from listening in – but that didn't include personnel walking down the hall.

After a few rings a gruff, drowsy voice answered. "Hello?"

"Authorization: NARRATOR," said Connors.

"Understood. One moment, sir," said the voice.

After a few minutes, there was a new voice on the phone. "This is EYEBALL. What do you need, sir?" it said.

"Anything on MONOLITH?" Connors asked.

"No sir, nothing yet, though I will keep you posted if he arrives here. Do you want us to contact him?" asked EYEBALL.

"Negative. Do not make contact under any circumstance. If something comes up, call for authorization first," Connors answered.

"Understood, sir. Is there anything else?" asked EYEBALL.

Connors wanted another update – two for the price of one. "Yes, what is the status of the conflict you mentioned in your last report. Is it anything to worry about?" asked Connors.

"It's escalating but at the moment, it appears to be contained to the island. As per your orders we are maintaining our neutrality. If any shots are fired, it looks like the Triad and the Vasilev Syndicate will win, though, thanks to the guns we delivered to them," answered EYEBALL.

"Good, we can't have the Cartel controlling the island. That would upset our interests there. Contact me immediately if MONOLITH shows up. Goodbye," said Connors before hanging up.

As he returned the phone to his pocket he wondered for what felt like the millionth time where Simon was. And what he was up to.

*****

If Connors' vision could have reached across the globe, he would see Simon on a relatively quiet sidewalk in Bangkok, returning to his hotel after breakfast at a small restaurant not far away. It was a cheap little hole-in-the-wall located in one of the city's shadier neighborhoods. As he walked, he passed a bar and felt an urge to go in and renew a bad habit. But no – he had sworn to never touch alcohol again after what it had cost him. He continued down the street lost in thought. Suddenly he felt a sharp pain in the back of his neck.

Simon instinctively put his hand at the point of the pain and felt an object sticking out of the back of his neck. He pulled it out and examined it under a streetlight on the pre-dawn sidewalk. It was a dart with a small hypodermic needle sticking out. Simon quickly looked around for his attacker, but his vision was already beginning to blur. His legs were weakening as well.

"Shit," Simon grunted as his legs collapsed. He fell forward onto the grimy sidewalk.

From his prone position, Simon heard a black car stopping behind him. With his quickly diminishing strength he turned his head and saw two blurry men getting out, one of whom held a dart gun. Simon tried to speak, but he sensed himself drifting off into unconsciousness.

The two men picked up Simon's limp body, put him in the trunk of the car and drove off.

Chapter 4

Into the Twilight Zone

Hours later, Simon woke up, still lethargic but aware of a sharp pain in his arms. When he tried to move them, he discovered they were chained together and above his head. Simon looked around, the cloudiness fading. He hung from a crane in the middle of a large empty warehouse, a solid steel chain around his wrists dangling him several inches off the ground. Struggling was pointless; the chain would be impossible to break. His gun and holster were gone.

His mind raced to figure out who had kidnapped him. *It wasn't Blacklist Protocol or some other agency like Silhouette – they'd just kill me. The Guild? The Networc? But then why haven't they killed me?* Simon wondered.

Suddenly the front door of the warehouse opened and three Chinese men walked inside. The oldest man had short gray hair and wore a black trench coat, vest, pants, tie and a white dress shirt. His face was worn by time, but his eyes were bright over a mischievous smile. The two younger men each wore white dress shirts, black pants, blazers and black ties. Simon assumed they were the old man's bodyguards.

The old man said something to the others; Simon's ears strained to pick out the Mandarin, but he was too far away. When the old man gestured to the door, the younger men clearly became nervous, but they left without a word. Once they were gone, the older man faced Simon. He walked up to Simon slowly, studying him from head to toe, his smile now gone.

"We make war that we may live in peace," said the old man calmly in English.

"Aristotle," Simon said, instantly recognizing the quote.

"Yes, yes, it is, Mr. Kane," said the man, obviously impressed.

"As much as I'd like discuss ancient Greek philosophers, I'm a little tied up at the moment," replied Simon wryly.

The older man grinned. "An extreme, yet necessary, security measure. We can't have you running off, can we?" asked the man rhetorically.

"Depends on who 'we' are," Simon retorted with annoyance.

"I suppose it does," replied the man.

Simon's shoulders were on fire from the strain. "Who are you? MSS, NIA?" he asked.

The old man shrugged. "Allow me to apologize for the rude method of contacting you, but it was imperative that I met you. I couldn't risk your saying no," said the man apologetically, in perfect English. "My name is Lin Yunao. I am the leader of the Heise She li Triad. Perhaps you have heard of us?"

Simon had indeed heard of the Triad; few people in his former profession hadn't, since the group controlled almost all organized crime in Asia, one of the largest and most feared criminal organizations in the world. Interpol and Simon's former bosses in Silhouette had countless files on them.

Members of the Heise She li Triad were known for their unique approach to displaying rank within the organization. The leader, known as the Mountain Master, wore the exact clothing Simon noted on the old man. Next in line were the Red Poles who wore the black trench coats, ties, pants and white shirts, but no vests. Their assistants were recognizable in white shirts only, with the same black pants and ties. The soldiers, referred to as 49ers and Blue Lanterns, wore white dress shirts, black blazers and pants, along with black sunglasses and their hair slicked back. Simon silently cursed himself for not realizing who they were when he saw them, as well as for being kidnapped in the first place.

"Good for you," Simon said sardonically. "So are you gonna hand me back over to the U.S.?"

Lin laughed. "Mr. Kane, the ten million dollar reward your people are offering is pocket change to me." He grew solemn. "You see, I have a little problem. If you agree to help me with it, I will help you with yours."

"And if I refuse?" asked Simon.

"Then you may leave here at once ... in pieces," Lin replied dryly.

"I'm listening," said Simon, not so much patient as aware that he was a captive audience.

"I thought so. Are you familiar with Sankan Island?" Lin asked.

"A little – it's an island in the Devil's Sea," answered Simon, shifting slightly to put pressure on a different area. "The Chinese, Filipinos and Japanese have been arguing over who owns it for decades. It's currently a haven for fugitives, international criminals, assassins and worse."

Lin seemed surprised by the answer. "Impressive; however, the island is not as anarchic as you think," he replied.

"That a fact?" asked Simon sarcastically.

Lin circled Simon slowly as he explained, "Yes, you see the city on the island is divided into three sections, each under the control of a different organization. The Vasilev Syndicate from Russia, the Rojas Cartel from Brazil, and yours truly operate via a mutual agreement that ensures a peaceful equilibrium," continued Lin.

"The big three," Simon commented.

Simon was surprised by this information. Sankan was infamous in the intelligence community for being a black hole where all attempts to infiltrate it seemed to disappear.

"Very astute, Mr. Kane. I believe it was your *Time* magazine that called us that," said Lin calmly.

"There a point to all this?" asked Simon impatiently.

Lin rolled his eyes like a frustrated teacher. "Americans," he muttered. "Last month, the Brazilians attacked us and the Russians. As a result we have been at war with the Rojas Cartel on Sankan Island ever since. Suffice it to say, their goal is to take complete control."

"So much for equilibrium," said Simon dryly.

"The Cartel's forces lack the discipline and weaponry that we have. With the aid of some members of the Assassins' Guild, we have had great success – unfortunately, when you push someone far enough, he snaps," said Lin.

Simon caught a glimpse of what looked like tears forming in Lin's eyes before the man brushed them away quickly. Tears in the eyes of the head of a major criminal organization? *That's surprising.*

"You see, a new factor has entered the conflict: my estranged daughter, Mai, my lotus blossom, born to us late in life, a miracle child," said Lin. "Three days ago she was kidnapped by the Cartel while en route to a relief camp in Belarus. They've threatened to kill her unless we surrender all our holdings on Sankan to them."

Bingo. "So what do you want me to do?" asked Simon, even though he knew the answer.

"Save her," Lin answered, holding his hands up in subtle supplication.

"Why can't you do it?" he inquired.

"They know our moves and our tactics. They'll kill her if we try to rescue her. They expect us to do just that, or send the Guild. You, however, would not be anticipated," explained Lin, his voice tinged with concern and desperation despite his efforts to hide emotion.

I am really getting tired of these chains, Simon thought. "Do you even know where they are holding her?"

"Yes, they are holding her in a stronghold on the island," Lin answered.

"Why did you let her go to Belarus without security in the first place?" asked Simon.

Lin sighed. "She would never have accepted it. My daughter is a pacifist, Mr. Kane. She abhors people like you and me, abhors the violence we inflict. She has devoted her life to helping others," Lin explained. "She has condemned me for my actions and hasn't spoken to me in years." Lin's eyes were sad as he looked up at his prisoner. "But she is still my daughter. I would move mountains for her. I am willing to offer you anything you want as a reward."

"I'm no mercenary," replied Simon.

Lin laughed. "On the contrary, Mr. Kane, the path of the mercenary is that which you must now walk. Your people have abandoned you and you fight with no army. A mercenary is exactly what you are," he pointed out.

Lin began to circle Simon again. "I sympathize with your predicament, Mr. Kane, but I am not offering you money in exchange for your services, if that is any consolation. I offer something even more valuable, I am guessing: information on the men who killed your wife. The Networc! With our vast resources, we can help you find them," explained Lin.

Simon was surprised. "What do you know about the Networc?" *Or about my wife?*

Lin stopped once more. "We know enough! The Networc arrogantly and foolishly once tried to bend us to their will. When we refused, they killed *my* wife. We have been enemies ever since," said Lin. "However, they are elusive and hard to track down. As you know." Lin smiled up at Simon. "But I assure you that we will not only find them, but also that we will recruit a team to help you destroy them. In exchange for rescuing and guarding Mai. Quid pro quo, as they say."

Is Lin lying? Does it matter? Simon's mind reeled.

"Like you, Mr. Kane, I used to serve my country as a spy. I have done horrible things in the service of my people and I deserve whatever horrid fate awaits me. My men also. But my daughter … my daughter is truly an innocent," continued Lin. "Think what you will of me, but Mai is a humanitarian who has helped hundreds of people in war-torn countries. Will you save my daughter? Will you protect her while I assemble a team to help you find the Networc?" Lin asked.

So not just the savior, a babysitter too.

"Protect her? For how long?" Simon inquired.

"Six months, Mr. Kane. I have other enemies beyond the Networc and the Cartel. They have already killed my wife, but they will not have my daughter!" Lin answered. "Saving her is the immediate need, but then she must have a bodyguard to *keep* her safe."

"And you figure I'm it?" replied Simon.

"Precisely." Lin looked up anxiously. "Will you do it?" he asked.

Simon thought about it and sighed. *Hell of a job interview.* But it was kind of nice to meet someone else that had suffered at the Networc's hands. Someone else who could understand how he felt. *Fuck it.* "I have three conditions," said Simon, bending one hand to extend his fingers as he spoke. "One, I will not betray my country's secrets."

Lin frowned, offended. "Mr. Kane, I would never ask a fellow soldier to betray his people.

American secrets are of no interest to me. What are the other conditions?" asked Lin.

"I will not kill innocent people," said Simon stretching out a second finger.

Lin stood a little taller and eyed Simon harshly. "Mr. Kane, you confuse me with some terrorist butcher. I am a soldier; soldiers do not kill innocents unless there is no other choice. I would never ask you, or any of my men, to kill the innocent. Only the guilty. Now then, what is the third condition?" Lin asked.

"After I get what I want, I'm gone," Simon answered.

"Agreed," said Lin. "You may leave – and I will leave you alone unless you betray me. Do we have a deal?"

"Yes," Simon replied.

"Excellent!" Lin pulled a remote out of his pocket and pushed the release button.

Simon landed on his feet as the heavy chain landed next to him, but the hours hanging had numbed them; he sank to the ground. Simon quickly unwound the chain from around his wrists and tossed it aside. Simon felt relieved to be free as he rubbed his wrists and stretched his arms, thankful for the painful tingles as blood rushed into his legs and feet.

Lin extended his hand to Simon, which Simon grabbed. Lin pulled him up and looked at him steadily.

"So, what now?" asked Simon, opening and closing his hands while stomping first on one foot, then the other.

Lin nodded slowly. "Now, we prepare," he replied.

Chapter 5

The Other Side of the Coin

Simon followed Lin out of the warehouse to a black stretch limousine parked outside. As they approached the car, the driver got out and walked toward them. He reached into his breast pocket and pulled out Simon's holster with his pistol inside, offering it to its rightful owner. "Thanks," Simon said, pulling the pistol out to check it.

The driver nodded in response before opening the left rear door of the car, gesturing for Simon to enter after Lin.

"You'll notice we cleaned your gun," said Lin as he watched Simon study it in the back seat.

"Gotta love Chinese hospitality," Simon quipped as he returned the Jericho to the holster, satisfied with its condition.

"You will find that I treat my friends far better than I treat my enemies," said Lin as Simon removed his coat, slid the holster on and somewhat painfully slipped his coat back on.

"I'll bet. But where are my bullets?" Simon asked.

"A security precaution; you'll receive your ammunition on the island," replied Lin, leaning forward to tap on the driver's shoulder, a signal to start the car.

"You're the boss," Simon answered dryly as the car began to move.

"I must ask: Why do you insist on wearing that old trench coat?" asked Lin.

"For good luck," said Simon dismissively.

"Of course," muttered Lin with a roll of his eyes. The men said nothing for a few minutes as they passed more warehouses and entered a more congested highway.

"Where are we going?" Simon asked finally.

"The airport. I have a plane waiting to fly you to Sankan along with one of my most trusted men – a man named Deng. He will fill you in on the specifics," Lin answered as the car wove seamlessly in and out of traffic.

"Sounds like a plan. You must have been pretty sure I'd accept your offer," noticed Simon. Outside, it began to rain.

"I make it a point to study people I may want to use. I've been watching you for some time, Mr. Kane. I know you, which is why I have not offered you a drink. You gave up the bottle some time ago," Lin answered.

Simon nodded. "Smart, though I'm curious about something you said also – you used to be a spy, then you became a criminal. What happened?" he asked.

Lin sighed. "Mine is a tragic tale not unlike your own, Mr. Kane," he began. "Years ago my men and I were part of the Ministry of State Security's elite black ops division known as Dragon 6. Much like our counterparts in other countries, Dragon 6's members were taken from the best of the best of the People's Liberation Army's Special Forces."

"I was the leader of the division," Lin continued. "For ten years we safeguarded the People's Republic from any and all threats, foreign and domestic," he explained.

Lin paused, reached into a small refrigerator and pulled out an expensive bottle of scotch and a glass. Simon ignored the smell of the drink and avoided looking at it as best he could.

"To this day I don't know who ordered it," Lin talked as he poured his drink, "but one night we were suddenly attacked by our brothers in the PLA and MSS. What was once a force of a thousand highly trained commandos was reduced to five hundred."

Simon was fascinated. Information as to the origin of the Heise She Li Triad was sketchy, even to Silhouette. "So then what?" he asked.

Lin lifted his glass in salute before taking a sip before continuing. "We did the only thing we could do: flee to Hong Kong, which as you know was under British control at the time," he answered. "I'll be honest, Mr. Kane. While we were in hiding, the thought of defecting to the Americans or the British did occur. In the end, we couldn't bring ourselves to betray our country, however." Lin took another sip of the scotch.

The smell of the open bottle was not lost on Simon. He studied the raindrops making patterns on the window beside him as Lin droned on.

"Call it patriotism or loyalty, I don't care which," Lin said, "but as we figured out what to do next we concluded that there was one place where our skills could be put to use: organized crime."

Lin's voice was soft and even, but Simon listened as the man continued. His musings might prove useful in the future.

Lin warmed to his topic. "Before the revolution, the Heise She li Triad controlled all of China. *After* the revolution, Chairman Mao set his sights on the Triad. He drove them out of China and into Hong Kong and Taiwan. The Triad was a mere shell of its former self, and thus ripe for conquest." Lin swirled his glass a little, smiling at Simon, knowing the effect the smell must be having on a former alcoholic.

"We watched and studied the Triad for almost a year until finally striking," said Lin. He turned the glass up and drained the last drops. "Out of all the opponents we had fought, the Triad was the most pathetic, whore-mongering, drug-addicted bunch of mobsters with no discipline whatsoever that we had ever come across. It was almost too easy to take over, removing all traces of the old guard." Lin placed his empty glass back in the mini-fridge.

"Impressive. So I guess that made you the new Mountain Master?" Simon asked.

Lin smiled as if flattered. "Yes. I, too, am impressed – though not surprised – that you are familiar with our hierarchy," he replied.

"Comes with my old job. Anyway you were saying...?" Simon encouraged the man to keep talking.

"Our victory would have been more impressive and meaningful if the Triad had been a worthy opponent, but ...," resumed Lin, his voice fading with implication. "We replaced the former leaders and began making changes."

Traffic was at a standstill, it seemed. *Life in the big city.*

"I kept the Triad hierarchy and nomenclature of Mountain Master mainly to appease the old Triad members who joined us," explained Lin. "Some call me the Dragon Head but I feel 'Mountain Master' has a better – how do you say? – *ring* to it." Lin smiled.

"No denying that," Simon commented.

"Very true. My men adopted similar titles as we expanded," replied Lin. "As Mountain Master, my first act was to establish Hong Kong as our headquarters. With that accomplished we began recruiting street soldiers."

Lin continued. "Once we had enough recruits, we put them through the same training that had made us into the warriors we are, while simultaneously planning moves to increase our power and reach. After about two years of recruiting and training, we were ready to begin," he said.

The car gave a little lurch then began to accelerate. Lin's pace also quickened, excited to share about his success. "Begin we did!" Lin's eyes were bright at the memory. "Within months we had forced the Yamaguchi-gumi Syndicate out of Taiwan and the islands," he explained. "Within two years we had crushed all opposition and had control of almost all organized crime in Asia!"

Lin frowned. "It was at this point that our biggest rival, the Vasilev Syndicate, contacted us – a complete surprise. They wanted to be allies." Lin paused, gazing out his window. "We accepted, though suspicious of their intentions. Everything was fairly routine after that … until the Networc demanded we surrender our territory to them."

Lin turned to face Simon again. "Naturally we refused. A few days later – to send a *message* – they detonated the bomb that killed my wife," explained Lin mournfully. "Mai was a teenager. What did I know of raising a girl alone?"

"How do you know the Networc was behind it?" Simon asked.

"They are the only people bold enough to commit such a brazen attack against us," hissed Lin. "Ever since then we have been at war,. You see we both want vengeance against a common enemy," he explained. "I'd say our wars are one and the same, wouldn't you?"

"The enemy of my enemy is my friend' – an ancient saying, and a true one," Simon answered.

Lin laughed as the car drove through the gate leading onto the airport's tarmac. "Ah, we are here," he said.

The car eventually stopped in front of a hangar. A private jet was waiting on the tarmac with a set of stairs next to the open door. In the doorway of the plane with a black umbrella was a man in "uniform" – black trench coat, black pants and tie, white dress shirt, black sunglasses and smoothed black hair.

"Some bird," said Simon drolly as he got out of the car and went around to the other side to better study the plane, ignoring the rain.

Lin rolled down the window to address him. "Deng will brief you on the flight, Mr. Kane, but be careful. Sankan Island is not to be taken lightly," the old man warned.

"So I keep hearing," Simon muttered as he turned away from the car and walked up the glistening, slick stairs.

The man in the trench coat balanced the umbrella with one hand and extended the other to Simon for a handshake. "Greetings, Mr. Kane," he said amicably.

"Deng, I presume?" Simon asked as he shook the man's hand. *A Red Pole*, he thought.

"Correct. I must say you're not what I expected," said Deng, covering Simon's head also with the umbrella.

"Most people expect two eyes," replied Simon slyly.

Deng grinned at the joke.

"When do we leave?" asked Simon.

"As soon as possible," Deng answered.

"Works for me," replied Simon.

Deng gave a little nod of salute to the limousine before closing the umbrella as they stepped inside. As Simon followed Deng, he wondered if he could trust him. Then again, he really had no choice.

Simon took in the fine details of the passenger cabin as he sat down on one of the buttery soft leather couches beneath the jet's windows. It was as plush as any penthouse suite in a five-star hotel with a minibar and television. Deng secured the door; outside, the ground crew moved the stairs out of the way so the jet could take off.

Chapter 6

Gliding over All

Once the jet was in the air, Deng stood up and poured himself a drink at the minibar and returned to his seat with the glass. He drank half of the glass as Simon watched, ignoring the voice in the back of his head telling him to pour one for himself.

Deng sat down beside Simon. "Mr. Kane, as the Mountain Master told you, I'll be your handler on this mission. Before we begin, do you want something to drink?" he asked.

"No thanks," said Simon.

Deng shrugged. "An American that doesn't drink – now I've seen everything," he said dryly. Simon grinned in response but said nothing.

Deng finished his drink in one gulp, then reached into his pocket, pulled out a phone and tossed it at Simon. Simon caught it with one hand, studying it, confused. "I already have one of these," Simon said as he held up the phone.

"Not one with a GPS, detailed maps and all the data you'll need to find Mai once on the island," said Deng. "In addition to that, we'll give you an earpiece communicator that will allow for instantaneous communication and updates."

Simon shrugged as he put the phone in his pocket.

"We're more than mere criminals, Mr. Kane. We are *professionals*. Each one of us is as highly trained and proficient as the rest," Deng continued.

"Yeah, Lin gave me the history lesson on the way here," Simon replied.

"I can assure you the Mountain Master was telling the truth," said Deng in a dead serious tone.

Simon decided to change the subject. "What's the plan?" he asked.

"At zero eight hundred hours Friday morning we will launch a coordinated invasion of the Cartel's territory," Deng explained as Simon listened intently. "However, at zero *seven* hundred hours, you will arrive at the house where they are holding Mai, codename: LOTUS, and rescue her."

"What's the exfil plan once I've got her?" asked Simon.

"Once you have her, press the red button on the phone's main menu. A helicopter will pick you up at the marked location and take you to safety. A successful extraction," Deng answered, as if it would be simple.

"You said 'we' – who else is in on this?" Simon asked.

"The Vasilev Syndicate will be joining us in the invasion," explained Deng. He remembered something else. "Oh, and incidentally, you should know that the Syndicate recruited a member of the Guild as well."

Simon wasn't surprised at this bit of news, but he was curious *which* member the Russians had tapped. "Who'd they hire?" he asked.

"I don't know the actual name but I do know that the person they hired is referred to as codename: KATYUSHA," replied Deng.

"Huh," said Simon dismissively, to hide his shock. "I thought they'd have hired BABYLON." He had not heard the name KATYUSHA in years. "Am I going to be working directly with – this KATYUSHA person?" asked Simon, catching himself. Instinctively, he knew he should act as if he didn't know her. *But I know her well*, he thought.

"No. KATYUSHA's mission is to neutralize a high ranking Cartel operative on the other side of the island from you," Deng said.

"We will have meeting later where you will be given more details regarding your part in this operation," continued Deng.

"What happens after the Cartel is taken care of?" asked Simon curiously.

"The Mountain Master is finalizing negotiations with the Vasilev Syndicate's Pakhan as we speak," answered Deng.

"That is none of our concern, however," he shrugged. "We are soldiers, not policy makers,"

"Glad to know my place in the order of things," Simon replied drolly.

Deng ignored Simon's tone and checked his watch. "We're almost there," he said, looking at Simon with satisfaction.

"Good to know, though I have a question: Does the Cartel have anything ... special ... I should be worried about?" asked Simon.

"Hopefully, you will be spared the wrath of their most dangerous weapons," replied Deng.

"'Hopefully'? That's not very reassuring, Deng," said Simon sarcastically.

"It'll have to be," Deng grunted.

"What do these guys have, anyway?" asked Simon.

Deng made a face. "We believe they have a few World War Two era tanks that they bought from Cobalt Incorporated," he answered gravely, "but fortunately, they are not on Sankan."

Simon's former employers, Silhouette, kept organizations like the Rojas Cartel under heavy surveillance since they trafficked in weapons, among other things. They were also allies of the Colombian terrorist organization FARC according to a report he'd read during his time at Silhouette. The fact that they had dealings with an arms dealer like Cobalt Incorporated did not surprise him.

"How do you know they don't have them on the island?" Simon asked skeptically.

"Simple – we control the harbor. And the harbor is the only place on the island where the Cartel could unload tanks," answered Deng cockily.

Simon was about to grill Deng for further details when the intercom interrupted. The pilot instructed them to prepare for landing. Simon noticed that Deng looked somewhat relieved at the announcement. "You seem glad to be here," Simon remarked as he looked out the window hoping for a glimpse of the island through the clouds.

"Why shouldn't I? I am the head of our operations on Sankan," answered Deng nonchalantly.

"I guess *someone* has to be the mayor, even of Hell," muttered Simon, still gazing out the window at the approaching ground.

Deng studied Simon quizzically. "Hell or Heaven, Mr. Kane, it can only ever be one or the other." He straightened up beneath the seat belt. "Anyway, once we land, a helicopter will fly us to our headquarters. Oh! Before I forget ... "Deng reached into an inside coat pocket and handed Simon the magazine for his Jericho.

I'll likely be glad to have these on the island, Simon thought as he loaded the ammunition into his gun just as the jet's landing gear touched down.

As Deng had predicted, as soon as they landed they were airborne again in the waiting helicopter. The chopper allowed for a more detailed view of the island. It was dominated by a small city known as Sankan City, or simply Sankan; almost all of the population resided there. Beyond the city, Simon could see what looked like a small mountain range while in the distance. A large mountain loomed over the entire island. In reality, the mountain *was* the island.

The men had been given helmets with microphones, but the roar of the engine still inspired volume. "Rumor has it the Japanese built a series of bunkers in those mountains during World War Two," shouted Deng.

"I'm not much for rumors," Simon replied loudly as he looked down at the city. War torn, the skyline was composed primarily of smaller two-to-three story buildings which appeared to be dilapidated. However the skyline was dwarfed by two massive and modern skyscrapers located side by side. The one on the right had a large structure on the roof topped by a pagoda, while the left building looked like a giant gray rectangular brick.

Deng leaned over and pointed in the direction of Simon's observations. "I see you've noticed the unique architecture," Deng said.

"It's kind of hard not to!" Simon answered dryly.

The helicopter slowed a little, making the shouting somewhat less necessary. "The architecture on Sankan is a combination of

Japanese, Chinese, Russian and Spanish designs," explained Deng.

"Hell of a combination" replied Simon.

"Quite," Deng gestured to the city. "The island was discovered by the Spanish centuries ago. They built a small village before leaving. Then during World War Two, the Japanese set up an airbase and began work on the city to house workers."

As the engine grew louder, so did Deng's voice. "The war ended before the city was finished. When the Syndicate, Cartel and the old Triad moved here in the mid-60s, they resumed construction. Hence the architecture," Deng said above the noise.

"And the two skyscrapers – what about them?" asked Simon as he nodded in the direction of the two mammoth buildings they were approaching.

"The one with the pagoda is ours; the other one is the Vasilev Syndicate's regional HQ. Both have 102 floors," said Deng.

In answer to Simon's unspoken question, he continued. "The Cartel is headquartered in a mansion on the other side of the island," Deng said.

"Is that where Mai is?" shouted Simon.

"No – hiding her there would be too obvious," Deng said.

As the helicopter neared the buildings, Simon got a better look at the Triad's headquarters. The pagoda structure on the roof held about two floors, he guessed, while in front of the structure he detected a small garden. Several people were waiting for them on a heltableton top of the pagoda.

Deng leaned in closer to Simon and grinned nonchalantly. "My personal residence," he said.

"Snazzy," Simon commented. As the helicopter hovered over the Triad's HQ, Simon shook his head. *What have I gotten myself into?*

Chapter 7

Dinner with the Damned

The helicopter landed on the helipad Disembarking, Simon and Deng were greeted by four Chinese men in the garb of the Blue Lanterns. Simon also noticed a black man standing at the edge of the helipad who wore gray-mirrored aviator sunglasses and a green camo jacket over his black shirt and pants.

"My personal staff," Deng said as he gestured to the Chinese men. "You'll excuse me, please; I must speak with them for a minute."

Deng casually walked over to the men while Simon leaned against the helicopter. He couldn't be sure, but Simon felt the black man had seemed surprised to see him. *Why?* He had no idea who the man was. Simon was about to walk over and speak to him when Deng finished talking with his staff only to exchange a few whispered words with the man himself.

Simon felt annoyed at being left out of the loop; he liked being watched even less. After a few minutes, the man in the camo jacket opened the door and walked inside as Deng turned and motioned to Simon to follow. Walking down a small flight of stairs, they were alone. The other man had apparently disappeared into thin air.

The space was dimly lit and stuffy. Curiosity got the better of him. "Who was that black guy you were talking to back on the roof?" asked Simon.

"His name is Ben Martin. American, ex-military. He runs a small delivery company down by the docks – the Flying Fish Trading Company. You needn't worry about them. They're neutral in the conflict with the Cartel," Deng explained.

The explanation was satisfactory enough, but it didn't explain why Martin had been surprised to see Simon. He decided not to mention this minor detail to Deng, who had enough to worry about. "So now what?" he asked instead.

"Are you hungry?" Deng asked.

"Yeah, I could go for something." Simon retorted

"Good," said Deng as they came to a landing. He opened a door for Simon and led him down a hallway.

They walked through another door and down a hallway to the elevator. Simon was glad to be out of the claustrophobic stairwell; at least the elevator was brightly lit. The doors opened at the ninetieth floor. Another hallway led them past what looked like hotel rooms on both sides.

When Deng reached Room 9008 he stopped and opened its door. The room was clean and though not lavishly decorated, it looked comfortable enough. There was a bed, TV and a desk with two chairs.

"This is where you'll be sleeping tonight," Deng said.

"It's a regular Holiday Inn, Deng," replied Simon.

"Your key card is on the desk and there's a suit for you in the closet," said Deng passively. "Dinner is at six-thirty on the fifty-fifth floor." As he left, he turned and smiled. "Just because we are criminals doesn't mean we cannot be civilized."

"I'll see you there," said Simon. Deng closed the door and Simon was alone. He checked the clock on the nightstand next to the bed: four in the afternoon. The black tuxedo in the closet was made to his exact measurements, from the finest material. *They thought of everything.*

Opening the curtains, Simon looked out at the city. He closed both blinds and curtains with a yawn, suddenly exhausted from his ordeal and the flight. He set the bedside alarm for six. *Thirty minutes to get ready for this dinner of theirs.* Although his expectations were low for island fare, he was so hungry he was sure he could eat whatever was served.

Simon took off his trench coat and hung it on a hanger in the closet. With another yawn, he stretched out on the bed, looking up at the ceiling. One last task before he allowed sleep to overtake him: Pulling the gun out of its holster, he slid it under the down-filled pillow before resting his head. Within seconds, he was asleep.

*****

In a car outside the building, Ben Martin pulled out his encrypted cellphone and selected NARRATOR from the contact list. After a few rings he was greeted with a gruff voice. "Hello, who is this?"

"Codename EYEBALL, sir," Martin replied.

"What is it, EYEBALL?" asked Connors from across the world.

"Sir. MONOLITH has arrived on the island. It appears that he is working with the Heise She li Triad," answered Martin.

Connors thought for a minute. *I knew he'd show up sooner or late.*

"All right. Maintain current status and continue surveillance. Keep me informed," said Connors.

"Yes sir," replied Martin as Connors hung up.

Martin put the phone back in his pocket and glanced upward at the Triad skyscraper before starting his car. As he left it behind, he came to the older, dingy streets of Sankan City. Even the looming conflict didn't deter the criminals of the city from walking the streets. Prostitutes and drug dealers littered the streets like the trash on the streets of Martin's native Chicago. *Hell of a place*, he thought as he drove back to the docks, back to the Flying Fish.

*****

The alarm clock buzzed like a fire truck's siren, jolting Simon awake. Siren silenced, he sighed and stumbled sleepily to the bathroom. A packaged toothbrush and toothpaste waited for him. He brushed his teeth, took a cold shower to rinse away the nap's effects and then got dressed. *Should I bring the gun along or not?* He was holstering his weapon when he heard a knock on the door.

A muscular Chinese man of medium build in a black suit stood in the hall. "Mr. Deng sent me to escort you to the dining room," he said.

"Of course he did," said Simon dryly. He grabbed the key card and checked the door lock before following the man to the elevator. Neither man spoke.

On the fifty-fifth floor the pair walked down a hallway, made a left down a corridor, and finally came to wooden double doors. In front of the doors was a tray table that had a lockbox on it. The man stopped and faced Simon.

"I have to frisk you, sir," said the man with an air of intimidation.

Simon raised his arms casually. "If you insist," he replied, as if he could not care less. *This can only go one of two ways*, he thought.

The man reached beneath Simon's tuxedo lapel and pulled out the Jericho 941. He dangled the pistol in front of Simon's face, scowling in disapproval.

"I thought it might liven things up," said Simon sarcastically.

Ignoring the joke, the man studied the gun with a cold, somewhat annoyed look. He checked it to see if it was loaded before looking up at Simon. "Weapons are not allowed in the dining room," he said sternly. "You will get it back after dinner."

"I suppose in a pinch, I could take someone out with a fork," Simon replied dryly.

Opening the lockbox with a key from his pocket, the man placed the Jericho inside. Simon caught a glimpse of two other guns already in the box. The man locked the box, returned the key to his pocket and opened the door, standing to the side to allow Simon to enter. "Enjoy your dinner, sir," he said.

As the man closed the doors behind him, Simon was greeted by Deng, also wearing a finely tailored suit. "Welcome, Mr. Kane! I am glad you decided to join us for dinner," Deng said warmly.

"Did I have a choice?" Simon asked, raising his eyebrow.

"Touché," replied Deng.

The dining room was both sizable and well decorated. Standing in the middle was a rectangular dining table with a spotless white cloth and sparkling dishes and crystal, service set for three. Beautiful paintings adorned the walls; a glittering gold chandelier dangled from the ceiling.

Already sitting at the table was a black-suited and bald, rather corpulent Caucasian man that Simon judged to be in his late fifties. Simon sat across the table from him while Deng took a seat at the end.

"Now that we are all here, I believe introductions are in order," said Deng. "Mr. Kane, allow me to introduce my colleague in the Vasilev Syndicate, the Russian mafia's head of operations on the island: Pavel Arbanov."

So this is the infamous Pavel Arbanov, thought Simon. According to the file Silhouette had on him, Arbanov had once been a renowned KGB agent. When the Soviet Union fell, he had been recruited by the Vasilev Syndicate, becoming one of the world's most wanted men. *And I'm shaking hands with him. Strange bedfellows.*

"Thank you for the gracious introduction, Deng," said Arbanov, his voice heavily accented. "I've always wanted to meet you, Mr. Kane. You have quite the reputation at Lubyanka Square."

"It was all a misunderstanding, I can assure you," quipped Simon.

The Russian grinned. "Indeed. I am curious, nevertheless. Would you happen to know anything about the death of a former SVR agent named Yuri Menshov several months ago?" asked Arbanov, the grin never leaving his face.

"Sorry, I've never been to Russia," Simon said. "Too cold for my blood."

Arbanov shrugged. "I suppose it does not matter. Menshov was a traitor," he said dismissively.

Just then several waiters walked into the room; three of them carried covered trays. While two waiters filled Arbanov's and Deng's glasses with liquor, another waiter filled Simon's glass with a brown liquid. He sipped it. His favorite – an Arnold Palmer, half lemonade and half-sweetened tea, quite non-alcoholic.

The other waiters placed a tray in front of each man, removing its lid to reveal steak, mashed potatoes and a small dish of steamed, sliced vegetables. The food's incredible smell made Simon's mouth salivate. Finally the waiters placed a bowl of rolls with a plate with butter in the center of the table before leaving.

"Quite a feast, Deng," Simon said.

"The Mountain Master instructed me to treat you as hospitably as possible," said Deng.

"Tell him I said thanks. It's been too long since I've had steak," said Simon as he picked up his fork and knife.

The steak was among the best Simon had ever had; the same could be said for the rest of the food. The next few minutes were devoid of conversation as the men enjoyed their meal.

As Simon took a drink of his tea, he glanced up at the paintings on the wall behind Arbanov, studying them. "Interesting paintings, Deng," he said. He pointed to the one on his left. "That one in particular looks familiar," he said.

"Ah yes. That one is one of my favorites," said Deng. He continued smugly, "You would not believe how bad the security is at the Tokyo National Museum."

"I'll just bet it is," replied Simon, returning to his plate. "What's up for tomorrow?" he asked, changing the subject.

"Tomorrow we prepare for the invasion," answered Arbanov.

"We have a state-of-the-art shooting range underneath this building, as well as any and all weapons you might need," said Deng.

"That's good to know," Simon said, his voice casual. He paused as he cut another piece of steak. "I've been wondering something, Mr. Arbanov. Why hire from the Guild? With the combined resources of the Syndicate and Triad, why ---"

"The Guild's members have their uses, as does everyone else," interrupted Arbanov.

Simon nodded as if in perfect agreement. "It's like they say, if you want something done right, get a professional," he said.

Arbanov popped a buttered roll into his cheeks and continued to talk. "You needn't worry, Mr. Kane. You and KATYUSHA's paths should not cross," he said.

Whenever she and I are in the same place, they usually do, thought Simon. "Good to know," he said aloud. *'Last thing I need right now is to run into* her *again.* Looking at his clean plate, he smiled. *Mom would be so proud.*

Chapter 8

Mirrors

After dinner the men left the dining room together and bid each other goodnight as the guard opened the lockbox and passed out their respective weapons. They went in three different directions. The guard did not accompany Simon, as it was apparently and correctly assumed that a man of Simon's spy stature would remember how to navigate the elevator and hallways leading him back to Room 9008.

Despite the nap, Simon was ready for sleep. He had closed the curtains and blinds to darken the room earlier, but walking into his room now, however, he smelled, then felt, a slight breeze coming from the window.

He could also tell that he was not alone.

As Simon reached for the light switch, a familiar voice with a seductive Russian accent came from the vicinity of the chair by the window. "How was dinner, MONOLITH?"

Simon whipped out his pistol, flipped off the safety and quickly aimed straight for the voice. "Show yourself!" he barked.

"Do I really have to?" the voice purred. "You know who I am."

"I wondered when I would see you again, KATYUSHA," said Simon, inching closer to the chair. Although he lowered the pistol, his finger remained on the trigger.

"Is that so?" the voice asked.

Simon holstered his pistol. "I've had a long day and I'm not in the damn mood for games."

"Clearly," said KATYUSHA, as Simon turned on the light.

Simon had never expected to see Sasha Molotova – former Red Curtain agent-turned-assassin – again. Codename: KATYUSHA. Years before, when he was a member of Silhouette, he had come into contact with her multiple times.

It had been years, but she was every inch as voluptuous as he remembered. Movie star beautiful, the tall blonde had the body of a supermodel with the muscle and agility of an Olympic gymnast. Like Simon, she had lost her right eye in the service of her country, covering it with a black eye patch, now also partially covered by her long silky hair.

She wore a black cat suit with long dark red boots, short dark red gloves, and a dark red belt. A dark red shoulder holster held her scoped Mauser C96 pistol; there was a knife strapped to her left leg. *Some things never go out of style,* Simon observed.

"Hello, Simon. Or would you prefer MONOLITH?" Sasha asked smugly.

"Either one," Simon said curtly. "So you're working for the Vasilev Syndicate now?" he asked.

"Just temporarily," Sasha said with the wave of a hand. "Initially I wasn't going to take this job, but when I heard the Triad had hired *you*, I couldn't believe it. I had to come see for myself."

"You couldn't believe what?" asked Simon.

Sasha smiled coyly. "That you had become a mercenary like me."

"This is only a temporary arrangement. I won't be signing up for membership in the Guild any time soon," Simon replied.

"Of course. And besides, I know why you are really here," continued Sasha.

"Oh?" replied Simon.

"You are searching for Sheila's killer," said Sasha. "And the Triad must be helping you."

"Perceptive as always, Sasha," Simon said.

"The benefits of my old job," Sasha purred. "So ... tell me how it happened?"

Simon was about to ask how she knew of Sheila's death when he remembered that Sheila's death had been announced on the news. She had become known as a popular author. Of course Sasha knew the *what*, but not, it would seem, the *how*.

"What does it matter to you?" Simon asked.

"I always respected Sheila as a fellow warrior and soldier," replied Sasha. "Even though we tried to kill each other several times." The look in her eyes and the tone of her voice told Simon she was telling the truth.

"The short version is that she was killed by a man called Counselor Black," Simon said.

"Counselor Black?" asked Sasha, shifting deliciously in the chair.

Simon nodded. "He was working for a group called the Networc. Ever heard of them?" he asked.

Sasha shrugged, "No. I'm sorry. I haven't had the pleasure."

Simon had been trained to detect deception, but all he heard in Sasha's voice was sympathy. He sighed. "That's all anyone seems to know," replied Simon, disconcerted.

Sasha's good eye was soft as she looked at him. "Even though we fought often, I must admit that you, Sheila, and Deon were some of the finest warriors I have ever met," she said sadly.

"She was the best," Simon agreed.

Sasha's smile hardened again. "Still, I always wondered what it would take to bring you over to my side of the fence," she taunted.

"Don't flatter yourself," Simon responded with irritation. "The only similarity between us is that we're both missing an eye."

Sasha laughed, but there was no joy in the sound. "You couldn't be more wrong, Simon. Whether you admit it or not, you and I are mirrored reflections of each other. Yin and yang. Both abandoned and forgotten by our countries, soldiers without an army," she said with a self-satisfied air.

"I am not a mercenary," Simon said evenly.

Sasha laughed lightly as she stood up and walked over to him; their faces were mere inches apart. He could smell her hair.

"Because you have a code of honor?" asked Sasha coldly. "A code of honor is a crutch that will do to you what it did to Sheila."

As he heard his murdered wife's name coupled with criticism, Simon's face grew serious. "I'd watch it if I were you," he growled.

Sasha relished in the victory – she had rattled the great Simon Kane. "Make me," she cooed, batting her eyelashes in challenge as she raised her left hand as if to hit him. Simon blocked it effortlessly, only to find that it had been a feint. She grabbed his hand.

Before Simon could react, Sasha lunged, causing him to fall backwards onto the bed. She jumped on top of him, her right hand clenching his free hand. Simon cursed himself for letting her bait him – still, he couldn't complain too much. He was, after all, in a decidedly intimate position with a decidedly beautiful woman. Sasha leaned so close that their noses just touched.

"You and me, in bed in a nice hotel room. Does this remind you of our first encounter in Prague?" Sasha teased quietly.

"Vaguely," Simon replied.

Sasha grinned at the lie. "Then allow me to refresh your memory," she said suggestively.

She kissed him on the mouth. They held each other in embrace for several minutes before her grip on his hand loosened. She wanted his hands free to roam now. Their hands explored each other's bodies while their passionate kisses never faltered.

Simon's hands found the zipper of Sasha's cat suit just below her chin. He pulled it down, revealing the black, front-hooked lace bra that restrained her ample breasts. She removed her belt and disconnected the straps of her lingerie in a swift movement as Simon unbuttoned his shirt. As soon as all their clothes were off, they melted into each other, slaves to their desires, everything and everyone suddenly fading to shadows.

*****

When Simon awoke in bed several hours later, naked and alone, he looked quickly around the room. Sasha was gone. He sat up, turned on the lamp by the bed, and rubbed his face. "Damn it, she did it again," he muttered, annoyed but far from surprised. He was also, he had to admit, more relaxed than he had been in months. That might be a good thing on the eve of a mission.

A cool breeze wafted into the room. The window was still open from last night. Walking across to it, he opened the blinds and looked out at the island view, specifically eyeing the Vasilev Syndicate's building opposite him. *That's where she is, I'll bet.* He blew a little kiss towards the skyscraper before closing the window.

Walking back to bed, he noticed a piece of paper tented on the nightstand. He picked it up and read the contents silently:

Thanks for bringing back some good memories, MONOLITH, I'm sure you remember Prague now.

Sasha Molotova

Next to her signature she had planted a bright red lipstick kiss. Simon grinned and tossed the paper into the garbage can next to the nightstand.

"Don't think I'll ever need a reminder again," Simon said to himself with a wry smile, turning to walk into the bathroom. *I doubt even a cold shower will help, right about now.*

Chapter 9

Teeth of the Lynx

It was four in the afternoon on Thursday; Simon was in the shooting range in the basement of Heise She li Triad headquarters. He had put close to six hundred rounds through his Jericho 941, accurate for the most part. It was an impressive range with an equally impressive armory down the hall holding what looked like a thousand firearms of various sizes and types. Simon holstered his Jericho and made his way to the vast assortment of killing tools from which he would select more weapons for use the next day.

Cabinets holding rifles lined three sides of the armory; on a table in the middle of the room were some fifty pistols in an assortment of makes and models. At first, Simon ignored the pistols; he preferred using his own Jericho as a sidearm. Then he realized it would be a good idea to carry an extra for emergencies. *Now's as good a time as any, I suppose,* he thought, walking to the table.

He focused on the smaller, more concealable models. Since this gun would be used in case of emergencies, the possibility of it jamming was unacceptable; he selected a model 60 .38 snub-nosed revolver. Hanging on the wall beside one of the cabinets were holsters. Simon grabbed an ankle holster and checked it to make sure that the .38 fit. Pleased at the results, Simon tossed the holster with the selected pistol inside, on the counter attached to the table.

He then approached one of the cabinets, carefully studying the assault rifles it held. Most of them were Chinese variants of either the AK-47 or M16, but there were a few German and Austrian rifles included, as well as some Israeli models. After a few minutes of considering all the options, he spotted a particular rifle he had a long history with – a Heckler & Koch 416 assault rifle. Simon had learned how effective it could be during his time in the Naval Special Warfare Development Group. Grabbing the 416, he slung it over his shoulder by its strap as he knelt down to take four magazines from the cabinet's bottom drawer and slid them into his pocket.

Holstered pistol under his right pants leg, Simon walked back to the range, surprised to find Deng practicing. Simon walked to the lane next to Deng and placed his guns on the table behind them. *I wonder if he knows about last night's reunion with Sasha?* He certainly wasn't going to bring it up.

Deng stopped shooting, holstered his pistol and joined Simon by the table. "Mr. Kane! I thought I'd find you here," he said.

"I never pegged you for a shooting enthusiast," said Simon as he loaded the HK416. Deng looked more like a businessman, also necessary for any well-run organization, of course, even a criminal enterprise. Perhaps *especially* for a criminal enterprise.

Deng smiled, "A humorous but false assumption, Mr. Kane. Before the betrayal, I was one of Dragon 6's most effective agents."

"Call me Simon," replied Simon.

"Well then … *Simon,*" Deng emphasized with a little bow. "I try to get in a little target practice at least once a day. I don't want to get *soft,* as they say."

"Smart man," replied Simon casually as he loaded the 416.

Simon's ever-present trench coat was not buttoned; Deng noticed the Jericho in its holster as Simon worked at the table. Deng eyed the pistol curiously. "I must ask – why do you use such a cumbersome weapon as your sidearm?" he inquired.

Simon looked over at Deng; he had been asked the same question many times in the past. It was a valid question – most spies preferred using smaller pistols that were more concealable. Unfortunately, these also boasted smaller calibers with less stopping power. Following the mission that cost him his eye, and his subsequent recruitment into Silhouette, he chose to carry the more powerful Jericho.

Simon pulled the Jericho out and looked at it, studying it as if for the first time. "It's a long story, but the short answer is that when you're hit with this, you stay down," answered Simon as he pulled the slide back.

"That's not what our intel says," Deng challenged quietly.

Simon stopped working. "And what does your *intel* say about my weapon?" he asked.

"That the Jericho was a gift from your late wife, Sheila Goodbody," said Deng.

Simon was not surprised to hear that Deng knew about Silhouette; he assumed that Lin had told him everything. He replaced the Jericho in its holster and pulled the .38 from its holster to load it. As he moved, he closed his eye. He could still see the image of Counselor Black's bullet hitting her in that Belarusian bunker three months ago. Simon sighed and looked at Deng directly.

"You guys really take your research seriously, and yes, when I lost my old Jericho on a mission, my wife gave me this one as an anniversary present," said Simon, patting the holster under his coat.

Deng's gaze was equally direct. "Forgive me. I understand your pain. We *all* treasure that which reminds us of those we have lost," he said.

Simon was suddenly irritable as he loaded the .38 and replaced it in the leg holster. "If you knew that already, then why did you ask?" he said with a frown.

"Truthfully," explained Deng, "I wanted to hear your explanation."

"What gun do *you* use?" asked Simon, desperate to change the subject as he shouldered the rifle.

Deng responded by pulling out his pistol and holding it up for Simon to examine. "QSZ-92, nine-millimeter," Deng answered. It was the standard issue side arm of the Chinese intelligence agency known as the MSS, and specifically, of its current shadow agency known as 49.

"I guess old habits die hard," Simon quipped.

Deng shrugged. "Very true, Simon," he replied.

As they turned to leave, Simon noticed a small metal armband lying on a nearby table behind an adjacent lane. Deng noticed it at the same time; his face contorted in mild annoyance. "Damn, he must have forgotten to return it," Deng muttered as he holstered the Type 92.

"What is that?" Simon asked.

"It's one of our little inventions," Deng answered as he walked over and picked it up. "It's a special wrist blade. You put the armband on your wrist ... flip your wrist back like so ... the blade pops out. Very useful for covert assassinations. One of my men must have left it," he explained.

"Very clever," said Simon.

"Here, try it," said Deng, tossing the armband to Simon.

Catching it in his right hand, Simon put the band on his left wrist and flipped his wrist back. A small razor-sharp blade popped out. "Ingenious," Simon observed as he studied the blade and armband more closely.

"Keep it," Deng said magnanimously. "A gift from one ally to another."

"It kind of reminds me of *Marathon Man*," Simon murmured as he returned the blade to its catch by pressing it against the wall.

"*Marathon Man?*" Deng asked in puzzlement.

Before Simon could answer, a sudden explosion above them rocked the building, the force of the blast knocking both men to the ground. "What the fuck was that?!" yelled Simon as he stood up and brushed himself off.

In Mandarin – angry Mandarin, no less – Deng yelled into his ear piece as he rose. Simon couldn't understand the voice at the other end of the conversation because it was so faint, but Simon could definitely make out a sense of agitation, and the report of gunfire. Instinctively Simon drew his Jericho 941 while Deng continued talking.

After what seemed to go on for far too long, Deng stopped yelling and looked solemnly at Simon.

"Well?" Simon asked impatiently.

"That explosion was a car bomb from the Cartel. To make matters worse, they've dispatched a death squad that is headed for us now," answered Deng.

"Fuck," muttered Simon.

With a look of determination, Deng pulled Simon's loaded rifle from his shoulder, cocked it and began to run out.

Simon put his hand on Deng's arm to stop him. "Where the hell are you going? If you get killed up there, I'll have no support for tomorrow. Lin's mission will fail. Mai will die," Simon reasoned.

Deng's eyes were fierce, but resolute. "I'm going to help my brothers fight. Let go of me or *perish*," he growled.

When Simon removed his hand, Deng sprang for the door. For a few seconds Simon stood in the range alone. "Ahhh, screw it," he muttered. He sprinted to catch up to Deng.

As he followed Deng up the stairs, the sound of gunshots grew louder, accompanied by the screams of wounded men. At the top they dropped to the floor and crawled to the door leading to the lobby – the focus of the shootout.

Simon rose and flung the door open. Several Triad guards, armed only with pistols and a few Uzis, were embroiled in a shootout with an equal number of Cartel soldiers using more powerful AK-47s. There were already a few bodies bleeding out on the lobby's gleaming tile floor, some injured in the blast, others from gunfire.

One of the Cartel gunmen aimed his rifle at Simon. Before he could fire, however, Simon jumped behind the information desk, and then sprang up to shoot his would-be killer in the temple. His target dispatched, Simon quickly scanned the chaos before him. *Where are you, Deng? There!*

Deng had ducked behind a couch beside three other Triad gunmen. Vaulting over the desk, Simon took cover behind a nearby column. When he leaned out scant inches, he spied a Cartel shooter running in his direction, but looking elsewhere. *That's it asshole, look over there a little while longer,* Simon mentally ordered. He flipped his left wrist backwards; the blade obligingly popped out.

When the gunman was close enough Simon jumped out from cover and jammed the blade into the man's stomach, supporting his weight for maximum effect, twisting the knife. Even as the man howled in pain, the life in his eyes faded. Simon pulled the knife out of the man's stomach and let the body fall to the floor.

Instantly, Simon aimed his Jericho at four other gunmen headed his way. As his pistol clicked empty he grabbed the dead man's AK-47 and returned to cover. He cocked the AK and fired short bursts at the remaining gunmen from behind the column. Deng and the Triad guards joined the firestorm as more Triad commandos arrived from the upper floors.

The next few minutes sped by. Cartel gunmen dropped like proverbial flies. Those who still could run, retreated to an armored truck. When no more living soldiers could escape, the truck raced away.

Out of danger for the moment, Simon tossed the AK on the ground and ran to Deng. As Deng yelled orders to his men they each, in turn, followed his instructions without a word.

"You okay?" asked Simon.

At first, Deng seemed confused by the question but managed to quip, "Yes, but those bastards got blood on my suit."

Just then a man ran up to Deng with a phone. He spoke quickly in Mandarin. Simon's language skills were rusty, but he was fairly sure that the phrase *Mr. Arbanov is on the phone* was in there somewhere.

Deng thanked the man, taking the phone and entering a heated conversation. Deng's aide ran off to attend to other duties; the wounded staggered off to get medical attention, presumably somewhere in the building. Bodies, far too many bodies, lay still.

The acrid, familiar smells of death and gun smoke filled Simon's nostrils. He walked outside for fresh air, but also to see the extent of the damage. What was left of the attacking car smoldered in ruin. Triad soldiers in all directions were putting out flames and carting off the more seriously wounded. *Is there even a hospital on the island?* Simon wondered.

Across the street, an ominous column of smoke billowed from what looked to be the lobby of the Vasilev Syndicate's building. *What the –* As Simon wove around stopped cars and debris to investigate, he heard his name called behind him and turned.

"Simon!" Deng yelled, jogging towards him.

"Yes?" shouted Simon, moving quickly toward Deng.

"That was Arbanov on the phone," Deng said breathlessly. "The Cartel attacked the

Vasilev Syndicate at the same time they attacked us."

Unbidden, a vision of Sasha fighting her way through the horde of Cartel gunmen clouded his mind. "And?" asked Simon. "How did it go?"

"Same as here: worse for the Cartel than their intended victims. The only difference, though, is that the Syndicate snagged a captive," Deng said gravely.

"Poor bastard," said Simon smugly. "I almost feel bad for him."

"Well, I don't," Deng replied, spitting with rage. "This attack changes nothing! Tomorrow will continue as planned." Deng handed Simon the rifle he'd borrowed. "Now if you'll excuse me, I must inform the Mountain Master of the attack."

"Deng!" shouted Simon as the man made his way back to the building. Deng turned around. "You've seriously never seen *Marathon Man*?" Simon asked, his somber face breaking into a grin.

Deng shrugged, unable to join Simon in a moment of levity, reeling under his responsibilities and personal grief. He had lost many friends. He walked inside, and Simon just stood there in the middle of the street, staring at his surroundings.

Smoke swirled through the air all around him from the burning car in front of him and the bomb-damaged building behind him. Wails from city people affected, injured and frightened mixed with the sounds of those who at least knew they were in a dangerous business, that such things happened from time to time. Simon wondered how many islanders had been caught in the crossfire.

Where is Sasha? Most likely, with her particular skill set, she was still alive. *What is she doing right now?* He wondered if he would see her the next day. Realistically, it seemed extremely doubtful.

After all, we're both just cogs in the wheels of others' machinations, he thought. Shrugging off the moment, he walked back to the damaged headquarters of the Heise She li Triad.

Chapter 10

Fire on the Horizon

At that moment, coming out of the doors of the Vasilev Syndicate building, was none other than Sasha Molotova, codename: KATYUSHA. The stock of her AK-74 assault rifle rested sideways on her shoulder, her hand still on the trigger. As Simon had done before her, she wanted to assess the damage both to the Syndicate's building and also to the Triad's. She was especially, *personally*, curious as to whether or not one particular person had survived.

Suddenly she saw Simon through the acrid haze entering the building. She grinned, not surprised that he had survived. For a split second she thought about calling out to him but chose not to; they had more serious matters to worry about. *Maybe I'll run into him tomorrow. Most likely not.* Their assigned tasks would place them at different parts of the city.

As Sasha studied her surroundings, she was pleased to see that the bodies of the dead belonged more to the Cartel than to the Syndicate. Bullets littered the ground. The air was thick with caustic smoke from the bomb-delivering vehicles that had crashed into the two buildings. She took a deep breath, filling her lungs with the biting smell.

Surrounded by fire, blood and the ominous shadow of war, Sasha was in her element. It felt like it had been forever since she had been surrounded by anything else. War and death seemed to follow her wherever she went, blurring and destroying everything around her. Even her memory was starting to blur and distort.

Some things remained all too clear.

Her childhood in the orphanages of Moscow was an unhappy miasma of sadness and poverty. There were happy moments – the solace she'd discovered as a teen in the sport of gymnastics, for one. Later, she had excelled in the Russian military, even considering the brutality of Spetsnaz training. Her gymnastics skills and determination had taken her far, but these good memories felt like they had happened a million years ago. She had seen so much pain, known so much pain. She had *caused* so much pain...

Some scars would never fade. Sasha had only to glance in the mirror, her eye patch a constant reminder of her final mission for Red Curtain. She had lost her eye battling agents of the terrorist organization known as Aquarius in Dagestan. High praise had been heaped upon her by her leaders. Then – utter shock and subsequent depression when Red Curtain discharged her. "You have but one eye; you are no longer useful to us." *As if I need two eyes...*

The Guild had not been so ... shortsighted. The IAG, or International Assassins' Guild, had recruited her almost immediately. A few years later, she would meet one of the few men to earn – and keep – her respect: Simon Kane.

Sasha closed her eye, savoring the memory of their night in Prague. She had once been told by someone whose name she'd long forgotten that people like her … and Simon … walk on the edge of an abyss. If ever they should fall into the abyss, they are lost forever.

The statement still resonated with her. She had been riding on the edge of the abyss her entire life, taking care not to look over the edge for too long, lest she fall in and lose herself to the horror.

Deep down, she knew that that wouldn't happen. Despite how she had chided Simon the night before, she too had a code of honor, taken very seriously: She would never kill a child.

Sasha didn't like to admit it, even to herself, but death and darkness had been a part of her since she joined Red Curtain. She relished the life of a mercenary. The thrills, intrigue and danger were as addictive as any drug.

"Quite a dust-up isn't it?" said a familiar voice in a Hungarian accent from behind her. She turned around as Orb Marius approached.

Orb was a tall man with short brown hair dressed in a zipped-up light gray Member's Only jacket, black pants and gloves, and brown shoes. His eyes were hidden behind the black lenses of aviator sunglasses. In his mouth was a lollipop, its stick jutting out of his mouth.

"It usually is on Sankan," Sasha answered.

"Yes, yes. You know, they say the battlefield is where all life's truths are revealed, where we are stripped down to the naked simplicity of the absolute," said Orb, bobbling the lollipop stick with his tongue as he spoke.

"I've never heard that saying," Sasha replied.

"I'm not surprised. My grandfather said that to me when he was talking about fighting in the Spanish Civil War," explained Orb.

Of the few times Sasha had been to Sankan Island, she had worked with Orb even fewer. He always struck her as more cerebral than the typical brute employed by the Syndicate.

"I wasn't aware there were Hungarians in that conflict," noted Sasha.

"The old bastard went there to fight alongside his fellow communists. When World War Two started, he returned to Hungary to aid the Soviets," Orb responded. "He always maintained that the happiest day of his life was when you people invaded in '56." Orb's mouth curled around the lollipop stick in a contemptuous sneer.

Sasha glared at him, angry at the insinuation. "I'm no communist. My people suffered under the USSR as well," Sasha retorted. Though born in the last years of the Soviet Union, Sasha had a healthy dislike of communism, knowing full well how it breeds poverty and suffering.

Unfazed by either her glare or her gruff response, Orb stepped closer and removed the lollipop from his mouth. He twirled the stick slowly between his fingers. "Of course not. You're with the Guild, correct?" Orb asked skeptically.

"I'm not sure that I like your tone," said Sasha.

"That's funny. Because I do not like *you, comrade*," Orb replied.

Sasha grunted, "At least the feeling's mutual."

Orb paused a few seconds to take in the damage in the street where they stood. "Unfortunately, when the festivities kick off tomorrow you, me and my people are going to be fighting alongside each other," he said.

"Your point?" Sasha asked.

"I just wanted you to know that I'll be watching you tomorrow. And not just because you're nice to look at," Orb leered as he pointed the lollipop at her.

"Then you better keep up," said Sasha as she grabbed the lollipop, dropped it and crushed it with her boot.

She'd said enough. Wishing to be rid of Orb's company, she walked back inside to make final preparations for the mission. She could hear Orb's cruel laughter as she left his side. Turning for a final glare she saw that he had reached into his pocket and was un-wrapping another lollipop.

*****

Unknown to the conspirators, their chaotic attack and its aftermath was being scrutinized from the other side of the island. Ben Martin and the rest of the Goon Squad had witnessed it all – the vehicles, the explosions, even the aftermath. Martin sat watching the live satellite footage on a computer screen while

Kenji Yamada, codename: SNAPPER, and Fiona Ramos, codename: BARRACUDA, stood behind him.

Kenji was a well-built man of Japanese ancestry from Honolulu, Hawaii; his short black hair was gelled in shiny spikes. He wore a dark red T-shirt over black and gray camo pants; his belt holster belied the fact that he was ostensibly in the fish business.

Beside him, Fiona was tall and slender. Of Cuban descent from Miami, Florida, she wore a white short-sleeved crop top over belted denim short shorts. Black fingerless gloves adorned her hands while a pair of goggles dangled from her neck. The right side of her head was shaved and on the other, her short black hair was combed over her left ear.

"Well … what the hell do we do now?" asked Kenji dryly, his arms crossed.

Martin swiveled his chair around to face them.

"Yeah, Ben, you're the boss. What do we do?" inquired Fiona.

"Nothing yet," answered Martin.

Kenji and Fiona exchanged a look of confusion then stared back at their seated leader.

"Why?!" Kenji asked. *Action warrants response*, he thought.

"Our orders are to *surreptitiously* support Simon. With the Triad and the Syndicate counteroffensive tomorrow, though, things might get hairy," explained Martin.

"That's tomorrow?" Fiona asked in surprise.

"Yep," muttered Martin.

"See, this is why you have to pay attention, Fiona," Kenji said smugly.

Fiona scowled at him, dramatically extending a middle finger to scratch her cheek. The movement was not lost on her partner, who simply rolled his eyes in response.

Ben ignored the transaction. "Deng and Arbanov assured me that we are under their full protection. We aren't in anyone's crosshairs anyway," said Martin, adding "Yet" as he leaned back in the chair and swiveled slightly back and forth in thought.

"That's a first," said Kenji.

"What about Noam and the Blue Marble?" asked Fiona. The operation was fairly stripped down, maintaining clean lines, but complications were always possible.

"Noam's locked up tight in his place. Deng told me the Marble is under Triad protection as well," Martin answered.

Fiona chuckled. "That's good, 'cause if they go down, where would anyone get a decent gun or drink on this rock?"

Ben gestured to the stack of crates along one wall. "Still, if the shit starts flying our way we can defend ourselves." The crates marked FRESH FISH actually contained automatic weapons, rocket launchers and their own private cache of firearms, all of which had been reported as "missing" from several American military bases.

"Fuckin' A," Fiona replied. "And if things get really bad we can always bug out – take the *Rumrunner* and do some fishing while these assholes kill each other."

Fiona referred to their primary delivery vehicle: a modified Grumman HU-16 albatross seaplane. They'd dubbed it the *Rumrunner*, hearkening back to the days of Prohibition when illicit liquor was shipped in Caribbean waters.

"That doesn't take care of the *Simon* situation, however," said Kenji.

Fiona punched him good-naturedly. "Kenji, you are no fun," she said with sarcasm.

Martin sighed and swiveled back to the computer monitor. "We'll figure something out. Besides," he muttered, "Simon Kane can take care of himself."

*****

That night one of Triad's lower-ranked members escorted Simon from his room to meet with Deng. The man was tall and well-built, somewhat formal looking in the mandatory white dress shirt and black blazer and pants. Simon could tell the man and his comrades resented him being there – nothing overt, but they were not effective in concealing their disdain. He cared little for their opinions; he was not there to be liked.

The elevator descended, but it did not stop at the lobby. Instead, the display indicated that it was going underground. When the doors finally opened Simon followed his escort down a short hallway to another door. The man opened it, gesturing for Simon to enter alone.

As he did, Simon was immediately stunned by the sight he encountered. For a second he thought he was standing inside Mission Control at NASA. A polished steel railing overlooked a large room in which four rows of tables with computers were manned by technicians facing a large monitor screen on the wall. At the moment, the screen showed a map of Sankan Island with key sites highlighted in different colors.

"Impressive, isn't it?" asked a familiar voice.

Simon turned to find Deng standing behind him.

"Quite impressive. What is this place?" Simon asked.

Deng held out his arms proudly. "This, my friend, is the nerve center of all of our operations on Sankan and far beyond. Here we will coordinate tomorrow's invasion," he answered.

"Hell of a setup," said Simon.

"This is nothing; you should see the one at our main headquarters in Hong Kong!" Deng patted Simon on the back. "But enough of such matters – come with me." Deng gestured for Simon to follow him into an enclosure on the edge of the control room.

The smaller room contained a large wooden table and wall screen. Underground, with no windows, even the bright fluorescents overhead struggled. Seated at the desk was a younger Chinese man with glasses, wearing a white dress shirt with black pants and tie. *They just aren't much for personal expression here,* thought Simon wryly.

The man looked up from a tablet and adjusted his glasses as they entered.

"My assistant, Mazin Ho," announced Deng by way of introduction.

Simon shook hands with Mazin before sitting down across from Deng.

"You know the broad strokes of tomorrow's mission but now we go over specifics," Deng told Simon. "Mazin? If you please ..."

Mazin stood, walking over to the screen. As he tapped a point on his tablet, a map of

Sankan instantly appeared on the screen with several highlighted areas. One was in black, marked L; the other three were marked with blue Xs. Simon couldn't help but feel like he was back in the briefing room at Silhouette's headquarters.

"The L represents Mai, call sign LOTUS," explained Mazin.

"Sorry to interrupt," Deng said, turning to Simon, "but this reminded me. When you contact me in the field the call sign is RED POLE. Similarly, we will refer to you as – "

"MONOLITH," Simon cut him off.

"Of course," Deng replied with a little nod. He was not surprised that Simon chose to use his old codename from Silhouette.

"Continue, Mazin," said Deng.

Mazin gave the slightest of bows as he resumed. "The blue X's are friendly interests that have chosen to remain neutral," explained Mazin. "You cannot expect any assistance from them, but they will also stay out of the fray." He pointed them out specifically. "This is the headquarters of the Flying Fish Trading Company and *these* represent Noam and the Blue Marble," Mazin continued.

"Question," said Simon, raising his hand for attention.

"Deng mentioned the fish people earlier. Who are those last two?" Simon asked.

"Noam is an Israeli arms dealer, the only one we allow to do business on the island. The Blue Marble is ... a local bar," answered Deng.

"A bar?" Simon replied in surprise. *A bar important enough to include on a high tech map?*

"Yes, it serves as a 'watering hole' for the men. Both we and the Russians have a stake in it," Deng explained.

"Riiight," said Simon, not entirely convinced.

Mazin cleared his throat. "Anyway, tomorrow morning at oh-eight hundred, we will commence with the invasion," he explained as he pressed another area on the tablet.

Suddenly a wave of red washed over the island on the screen with a counter at the top that began counting down from eight o'clock a.m. to nine o'clock p.m.

"Our forces will march across the city and force the Cartel's people out. We predict complete success by twenty-one hundred hours Saturday night," Mazin explained.

"So your plan is to just storm them out?" Simon asked.

"Yes," Deng answered. "The Russians devised it."

"I'm not surprised; tell me about Mai," Simon replied.

Mazin used the tablet to bring up a picture of Lin's daughter on the screen. The picture had been taken in what appeared to be a Red Cross relief center in the Middle East. Her appearance reminded Simon of a librarian. *More attractive than most of the ones I've seen, though.*

"Mai is a twenty-five-year-old with no combat experience and an underlying philosophy of pacifism and humanitarian work," said Deng.

"That might make her a liability," observed Simon.

Deng's face was stern. "Mai's rescue is your absolute priority. If anything happens to her, your life is forfeit," Deng explained.

"Duly noted," Simon said with a little salute, "but what makes you think she's still alive?"

Deng and Mazin looked at each other.

"Don't tell me you guys are basing the mission solely on hope," said Simon flatly.

"If she is dead, you will notify us and bring her body to the extraction point," answered Deng.

"Got it." Simon leaned forward. The adrenaline was starting to kick in as it always did before a mission. "What about the extraction point?"

"Once you have her, you will bring her *here*," Mazin explained as he touched the tablet; a green circle appeared on the screen. "This where the helicopter, codename: DRAGONFLY, will pick you up and fly you to a ship. The *Zheng* is docked not far from here," he continued.

"The *Zheng* will take you to Taiwan. From there you will fly to Hong Kong," Deng explained.

"Wait ... a ship?" asked Simon curiously. "There's an airport here. Why not just use that?"

Deng sighed in annoyance. "Three reasons: One, the Cartel would be waiting to ambush you at the airport in Taiwan, which would bring undue attention to the mission. The harbor is much quieter and more controllable," began Deng.

"Two, the airport is considered neutral territory since we all use it. Three, if the Cartel followed you there, the airport could sustain damage which would inhibit our use of it in the future," Deng continued. "Satisfied?"

"Not even remotely, but I doubt I have a say in the matter," grunted Simon.

"Smart man," Deng acknowledged. He nodded to Mazin. "You most likely won't encounter them, but you should know that the streets of Sankan City are home to a street gang called the Smiling Boys." Deng elaborated as Mazin brought up a picture of one of them on the screen.

Simon studied the picture of a young man in his early twenties. Asian descent, probably Vietnamese. Long, scraggly hair; dressed in rags. His most distinguishing feature, though, was the large unnatural "smile" that had evidently been achieved by cuts on the sides of his mouth with a knife, creating ugly scar tissue.

"Creepy," murmured Simon.

"They mostly stick to harassing the people in the city ... who will most likely be hiding from us. We believe the gang will stay out of sight as well, but if you happen to encounter one of them, it's best to shoot first and ask questions later," replied Deng soberly.

Simon nodded slowly. "I imagine I'll be doing a lot of that," he said.

Deng stood. He and Mazin exchanged quick bows before he gestured to the door. "Yes, Simon, I imagine you will. But for now I would like you to get some sleep, and prepare for tomorrow," said Deng.

Chapter 11

Invasion of the Hood

It was early Friday morning. Simon Kane was in position across the street from the rear entrance of the building where the Cartel was holding Mai. It was a dirty unassuming two-story with a back door which, according to Deng, led to the kitchen. Simon wore his trench coat over a black short sleeve buttoned shirt and dark green pants. He sat in the car the Triad had provided, an ugly black thing that looked like it belonged in a junk yard. Deng had insisted he drive it, though – it was fast, armored and unassuming.

Far cry from the sports cars Silhouette gave me, thought Simon as he waited for Deng's signal to move in. His HK416 rifle lay on the front seat next to him. In the distance, he could hear the echoes of gunfire and explosions, the opening salvos of the Triad's and Syndicate's assaults on Cartel strongholds. Just like Deng said, the streets of Sankan City were devoid of people. It was as though they could see the storm coming, deciding to hide in their homes rather than risk getting caught in the crossfire.

Fewer civilians on the street meant less collateral damage – always a good thing in Simon's thinking. He wondered briefly what Sheila would think of his part in the mission, all in the name of revenge. He brushed the thought aside quickly, knowing that if circumstances were reversed – if he had been killed that day in Belarus – she would do the same thing.

How much longer, dammit!? thought Simon as he checked his watch again impatiently. On the surface, the plan was simple enough: Rescue Mai, head to the park where DRAGONFLY would pick them up and fly them to safety. *Even the best-laid plans of mice and men can go awry,* Simon thought pessimistically.

He checked again for guards outside the compound – still no one. Reaching into his coat pocket for the phone Deng gave him, he brought up the map of the island that was tracking the progress of the Triad and the Vasilev Syndicate via satellite updates in real time. Several of the Cartel's drug labs, cash houses and counterfeiting factories were already destroyed.

"MONOLITH, you are go for rescue, over," buzzed his earpiece communicator, a direct line to Deng. From the Triad building, Deng supervised their side of the attack operation.

"Roger that, over and out," Simon replied quietly as he pushed the "send" button. "Finally," muttered Simon, after terminating the transmission. He was relieved for the waiting to be over.

Simon returned the phone to his pocket and checked his weapons a final time. Cocking his HK, he got out of the car and closed the door without a sound. Quickly he ran across the street with his rifle drawn. In seconds he was in front of the back door. *Locked.* Old and wood, it offered no resistance as he kicked it open. Slowly, his senses primed and ready for anything, Simon walked inside.

Deng's Intel was correct, which boded well. The kitchen was filthy and odorous. A ramshackle table and two rusty metal chairs sat in the middle, while on the left wall was the door that led to the basement. On the table were several syringes and mostly-empty bottles of alcohol. Simon looked away from them, ignoring the temptation to take a sip. Every fiber of his being was focused only on one thing: the mission.

Angry voices yelled upstairs in Portuguese and Simon paused to listen. Just then, the basement door opened; Simon spun around at the sound, aiming his rifle at the man who opened it. The man lunged at Simon and pinned him against the refrigerator, causing Simon to drop his rifle.

The man's hands, tightly wrapped around Simon's throat, began to squeeze. Instinctively, Simon placed his own hands over the man's wrists, maneuvering for advantage.

They had grappled for several seconds when Simon remembered Deng's gift. Simon let go of the man with his left hand and flipped his wrist backwards to free the blade.

Simon jammed it into the man's neck and pulled it out. The man let go and grabbed his own neck as blood began to pour out. With his other hand, the gunman reached for a pistol, but Simon simultaneously punched his face and kicked his stomach. The man fell backward through the open door and down the stairs.

Simon chuckled as he bumped the knife back into the armband. "Deng was right – this *does* come in handy!" he muttered. As he knelt to pick up the rifle, he heard the sound of men rushing up the stairs. Running to the side of the doorway, he peeked around the corner and spied two furious Brazilian men with AK-74s running up the stairs to avenge their comrade.

Simon aimed his rifle at the men, firing two short bursts at each of them. They fell down the stairs, dead. Simon walked over the bodies and down the stairs cautiously, aware there may be more gunmen below.

At the bottom of the stairs was a short hallway with a locked door at the end. Simon ran to the door and shot the lock, flinging the door open, ready for anything on the other side. The room was small and dimly lit, furnished only with a small bed, table and chair.

Sitting in the chair was a young Chinese woman with long black hair. She wore a simple white t-shirt and blue jeans. The magazine she had been reading was still poised in her hands, but she looked at him without fear.

"Hello," she said casually. Calmly, as if not surprised to see him.

"Mai Yunao?" asked Simon brusquely.

"Yes," Mai answered with an air of disinterest. "My father sent you, didn't he?" she asked.

Throughout his illustrious career, Simon had been involved in many rescue missions. Hostages tended to react to the sudden appearance of their rescuers with either fear or elation. Until today, no hostage in Simon's experience had ever reacted with such complete nonchalance.

"Yep, now c'mon!" Simon ordered.

"What is your name?" she asked.

"What?" Simon replied, confused.

Mai sighed. "You have a name, right?" she asked. "I would like to know it."

"Simon Kane," he answered bluntly.

Mai slowly put down the magazine, stood up and walked to him. "Well, let's go then, Simon Kane," she said, her voice still cold and distant. It was as though being kidnapped and rescued was nothing remarkable whatsoever.

"Yes, ma'am," Simon replied.

A loud voice barked in English from the top of the stairs. "Stop and drop the damn gun!" Simon heard the distinctive cocking of two automatic pistols and knew immediately who it was – the two angry men from upstairs.

"You wish," muttered Simon, silently moving closer to the bottom of the steps, still unseen by the men.

In one swift motion Simon lunged forward and fired a short burst from his rifle at the two men above, killing them both. When he looked back at Mai he was surprised that her impassive expression had now given way to a combination of sadness, disgust and horror.

She stepped forward and gazed on the now *four* bodies. "Poor souls," Mai said quietly.

Must have Stockholm syndrome or something,
thought Simon. "You can send them a get well
card later – let's *go!*" he snapped.

Mai followed Simon out of the building
without another word. Once outside, though,
she ran beside him to the car, settling into the
front passenger seat beside him. After tossing
the HK in the back seat Simon called Deng on
the phone.

"RED POLE, I have LOTUS. She is in good
condition. Heading to extraction point, over,"
said Simon, his eyes on Mai. She should be
relieved, ecstatic, rejoicing in her freedom.
Instead, she looked sullen and petulant.

"Roger that, MONOLITH. DRAGONFLY
is inbound, over," Deng's voice replied into
the earpiece.

Mai seemed to be studying the floor. "You
okay?" asked Simon.

Mai looked at him with anger and
confusion. "Why did you have to kill them?"
she asked accusingly.

"Why do you care?" replied Simon as the
car growled to life. Simon floored it, afraid
there might be others in the building about to
emerge at any second.

As they drove to the park, Mai broke the silence. "Why do I care? What kind of question is that? I care because they're human beings, dammit! They're people!" she cried.

"Yeah, really *bad* people who kidnapped you. Do you have Stockholm syndrome or something?" asked Simon.

That confused her momentarily. "Stockholm Syndrome? No, I don't have anything of the kind. But you didn't need to kill them. You ... you ... wait. *Who* the hell are you?" Mai asked.

"I already told you my name," Simon growled. "What do you want, my life story?" He fumed a little as they sped toward the park. "I'm curious, too – are you *always* this grateful when you're rescued?"

"Grateful?!" Mai answered angrily.

What a piece of work. Simon took his eyes off the road long enough to glare at her. "Yeah, as in 'I'm grateful you saved my life'," he said feeling just a tad bit unappreciated.

Mai shrugged. "Typical American, always expecting gratitude," Mai said dismissively.

"Oh, shit," Simon muttered in alarm.

"What now you're *offended* that I criticized your perfect hypocritical country?" Mai hissed in attack.

"No jackass ... *that*," Simon replied as he pointed to a Cartel roadblock at the end of the four-way intersection in front of them.

"Oh, shit," Mai echoed.

The street was blocked by four gun trucks each fitted with two .50 caliber Browning machine guns on the roofs. Cartel commandos flanked the trucks on motorcycles. From the looks of things, they were getting ready to open fire on Simon and Mai at any moment.

Chapter 12

Fury on Thunder Road

"Listen, just surrender. It's over," Mai urged as they neared the roadblock.

Simon had slowed his speed considerably, but they were still in forward motion. He looked at her, a cocky grin on his face. "Surrender? I don't know the meaning of the word," he said smugly. A plan was already forming in his head.

Before Mai could respond, Simon accelerated the car, hurtling full speed towards the Cartel's roadblock. The surprised gunmen at the roadblock aimed their guns at them and began firing.

"What the hell are you doing?" yelled Mai as bullets bounced off the windshield.

"Breaking the speed limit, for starters," replied Simon casually as the car rocketed straight at the armed roadblock in front of them.

Just as the car entered the intersection, Simon turned the steering wheel sharply to the left. The car skidded sideways into the roadblock and knocked two gunmen to the ground. Reaching swiftly into his trench coat, Simon pulled out a grenade and yanked the pin out. He tossed the grenade out the window at one of the gun trucks. Finally, he jammed his foot down on the gas pedal. The car shot forward away from the roadblock.

Giving Mai a quick glance to check on her safety, Simon could tell that she was about to speak. He held up his finger to stop her. "Shhh. Wait for it …," Simon said dryly.

Before Mai could respond the grenade exploded behind them, turning the gun truck into a ball of flame that reached out to consume the men surrounding it.

"Nailed it," said Simon as he breathed a sigh of relief.

"Are you insane? You could have killed us!" Mai screamed.

Simon shook his head slyly. "You know for a pacifist, you have quite a temper."

"What does a killer like you know about pacifism?" asked Mai accusingly.

"More than you think I do," Simon muttered.

Mai laughed without humor – part shock, part mocking disbelief. "You're just another gun-fetishizing American that's watched too many Schwarzenegger movies," replied Mai.

Simon's eyes narrowed as he drove. *Is Lin sure he wants this one back?* "Lady, people like me have given their lives in the pursuit of peace," he retorted. "And by the way, Kurt Russell is way cooler than Schwarzenegger."

For a few seconds, Mai said nothing. Finally: "Who's Kurt Russell?"

Simon looked at her in mock incredulity. "You never saw *Escape from New York*?" he asked.

"No," Mai said icily, shaking her head.

"Well, that's just wrong," Simon replied.

Suddenly a bullet shattered the rear window of the car, startling the both of them. Instinctively, they looked behind them to see where the bullet had come from. Approaching at considerable speed were three of the Cartel's motorcycle commandos.

"Shit, these guys just can't take a hint," Simon grunted.

"Where did they come from?" asked Mai, her eyes wide.

"Clearly I should have used more grenades," Simon muttered.

Simon could see them clearly in the rear view mirror now; he took a visual inventory. They carried MAC-10 submachine guns in one hand while steering the motorcycles with the other.

One of the gunmen fired a short automatic burst at them. Simon swerved out of the way, narrowly avoiding getting hit. Bulletproof windows could only take so many hits before giving way. He shot a look at Mai. Despite the dangerous situation, she wasn't hysterical. She instinctively ducked her head to stay out of the line of fire. When she looked back at him, the frightened look on her face quickly hid behind something else.

"What?! This isn't the first time I've been shot at," Mai said defensively.

Simon ignored the comment. "Take the wheel," he ordered.

"Wait … what?" Mai was confused.

"You heard me," said Simon, climbing into the back seat of the car as Mai grabbed the wheel and slid over.

Simon picked up the HK, cocked it and lowered the left rear passenger window. He fired at the motorcycle gunmen in short bursts, managing to hit one of the gunmen in the chest. As their comrade and his bike fell to the ground, the remaining gunmen swerved out of the way and returned fire. Simon ducked back inside the car and waited for an opening.

"Simon!" yelled Mai.

"What?" Simon asked, whipping his head around.

The pavement ended ahead at a fork in the road. A small building, perhaps a restaurant, stood just across from it.

"Which way?" she asked frantically.

A sudden idea came to him. "Make a right on my mark," Simon answered tersely.

Mai nodded, not knowing what else to do. The building was getting closer and closer, and the remaining motorcycle gunmen were gaining ground.

As they approached the turn Simon could see that Mai was worried. "It'll be all right, trust me," said Simon with a reassuring smile.

Mai nodded, feeling slightly less nervous.

"NOW!" Simon yelled.

Mai made a hard right. The gunmen tried to do the same but didn't react soon enough; they crashed into the building. Simon smiled at the sight, motorcycle parts flying in all directions.

"Huh," Simon mused. "Can't believe that that actually worked!"

"What?" exclaimed Mai as Simon climbed over the seat.

"Hand over the wheel, Speed Racer," Simon said.

"Gladly. Wait … what?" replied Mai as she moved over to the front passenger seat.

"Never mind. Where'd you learn to drive like that?" asked Simon once he was behind the wheel.

Mai beamed, her first genuine smile of the day. "Growing up in a city like Hong Kong teaches you a lot about how to handle cars," she answered.

"I'll bet," said Simon as they continued down the streets of Sankan. *Maybe she's not so bad after all.*

Chapter 13

The Dragonfly Death

Now that they were safe for the time being, at least, Simon allowed himself the luxury of checking the phone's GPS to see how far away they were from the landing zone. *ETA 15 minutes.* He smiled in grim anticipation. *It won't be long now! Return Mai, protect her for a few months and then the Networc is mine!* thought Simon.

As he returned the phone to his coat pocket, Mai studied Simon. "You're not one of my father's men, so you must be a mercenary," she observed.

"Your point?" Simon asked.

"How much is my father paying you for this? How much money is my life worth to that criminal?" said Mai grimly.

"He's not paying me with money. He's paying me with information," answered Simon.

Mai was surprised. "Information? What does he know that you don't?" she asked.

"It's personal, but look at it this way: Your life is worth a lot to him. Otherwise, I wouldn't be here," Simon replied quietly.

Mai looked out the window. When she spoke, her voice was abrasive with restrained emotion. "What happens between me and my father is our business. Not yours or anyone else's," she said.

"Fair enough, your highness," said Simon sarcastically as they pulled into the park entrance. There were no other cars parked inside. Although that put him at ease a bit, Simon knew not to let his guard down.

The park was little more than a garbage-encrusted square, festooned with detritus and refuse. Dilapidated buildings surrounded the square; perhaps one day long past it had been a healthy, welcoming place for families to gather and play, but no more.

At the edge of the park was a dead tree. In its center was a flat patch of grass big enough for a helicopter to land on.

Simon called Deng on the earpiece. "RED POLE, we're at the LZ, over," he said.

"Roger that, MONOLITH. DRAGONFLY is en route, over," buzzed Deng's voice in response.

Simon took his finger off the earpiece and looked at Mai. "Chopper's on its way. Let's go," he said.

"About time," muttered Mai.

Simon grabbed his rifle; they ran to the small patch of grass as fast as they could. As they approached, they heard, then saw, the helicopter as it came into view over buildings and trees. Simon and Mai watched it land, shielding their eyes from whirling debris uplifted by the rotors. Mai looked up and smiled when she saw the pilot's face. *I know him!* she thought.

Suddenly something flew overhead and collided with the helicopter. The chopper burst into flames with a thunderous explosion.

Mai and Simon backed quickly away, looking on in horror, unable to do anything as the helicopter spun around in flames like a great beast in its death throes. As it began to fall, Simon dropped his rifle and lunged at Mai to push her out of the way, covering her head as he lay next to her. The chopper zigzagged first one way, and then another, before finally crashing into the side of an old building, tail first. The ordeal had only lasted half a minute, but it had seemed to unfold in slow motion.

Simon and Mai looked up as the noise of the crash faded into eerie stillness. "Well ... shit," Simon grunted, at a loss for words. Their best hope of escape smoldered in ruin.

Simon stood up and held out his hand to Mai to help her up. Still in shock, she took his hand. "My glasses."

As she stumbled around in a daze, Simon located them on the ground beside his rifle. He brushed off most of the dirt before handing them to her. "Here," said Simon.

Mai studied them a moment, almost in wonderment. A helicopter had crashed before their very eyes, but her glasses were still intact. "Thanks," she said.

"You're welcome, Velma," Simon grinned.

She looked at him, puzzled. "Who's Velma?"

Before Simon could respond, a barrage of bullets kicked up the dirt around them. Simon looked around, frantically trying to find out which direction the shots had come from – no doubt the same source as the missile that had hit the chopper. It was now dead quiet, which meant they were reloading. *No time to reach the rifle.*

Simon drew his pistol. "Listen to me very carefully," he whispered to Mai. "We're gonna have to make a run for it." He pointed subtly to an alleyway on the far left of the park so the shooters wouldn't realize his plan.

"On the count of three, run to that alley. Ready?" Simon whispered.

"But the pilot! Maybe we can save him!" protested Mai as tears pooled in her eyes.

Just then, the shooters emerged from cover, only to face the staccato welcome of submachine gun fire. The shooters fell over dead. To their amazement, Simon and Mai could now see the pilot lying on his stomach on the ground. Smoke wafted from the barrel of the Type CSO6 submachine gun he held in his right arm. The man, who appeared to be around forty, was injured. Both his left arm and leg were broken; his face was covered in blood from multiple cuts on his face.

"Wei!" cried Mai, running to his side.

"It's been a while, LOTUS," said the pilot with a brave smile.

Mai propped him against the smoking wreckage of the chopper, but Wei ignored her. He looked straight at Simon. "American," said Wei as he coughed up some blood. "I don't give a damn how you do it … but get Mai the hell out of here. I'll hold them off as long as I can."

Simon nodded. The last request of a doomed man; he'd heard enough of them to recognize them easily.

"What? *No!* We can help you!" Mai pleaded.

"No … I would slow you down," replied Wei, wheezing a little as blood filled his lungs. They could hear more soldiers approaching. "Go!" yelled Wei.

Simon grabbed Mai's arm, roughly pulling her away.

"No, Wei please!" begged Mai, but they were already disappearing into the alleyway.

Wei smiled weakly as they disappeared, secure in the knowledge that his sacrifice would mean Mai's survival. He feigned death as the pursuers ran past the wreckage; he certainly looked the part.

"Cocky bastards," said Wei with a smug smile as he raised his SMG at them and fired.

Simon and Mai ran into the dingy alleyway, the sounds of Wei's sacrifice echoing in the background. They stopped and jumped behind a rusting steel dumpster. Mai crouched, tears silently running down her face. Pistol in hand, Simon rose slightly to check to see if they were being followed.

"We have to go back for him!" whispered Mai loudly.

"Sorry, kid – not a chance," Simon grunted back.

Before she could respond, the sound of approaching footsteps echoed in the alleyway.

"Shit," muttered Simon.

Two gunmen armed with AK-47s approached. When they spotted Simon peeking out from behind the dumpster, they raised their rifles at him. Simon fired two shots rapidly, killing the gunmen instantly.

"Gotcha," whispered Simon triumphantly as he quickly moved back behind their hiding spot.

The successful shots had also, unfortunately, blown their cover. Almost immediately they heard the yells of others heading their way.

"They're over here," yelled a voice in Portuguese from down the alleyway. The soldier's voice was soon joined by seven more of the Cartel, all eager to avenge their fallen comrades.

"Oh, shit," said Simon. "We'll have to run for it." He cursed himself for leaving the HK in the park; he lacked the firepower to square off against them. He sighed and thought, *If this is it, I'm sure as hell going to go down fighting.*

Simon aimed his pistol at the approaching soldiers and began to fire. Suddenly, a fireball seemed to come out of nowhere before exploding in front of the soldiers, killing most of them. Those that survived were quickly dispensed with by gunfire from somewhere above.

Surprised by the unexpected rescue, Simon instinctively swung around and pointed his Jericho up at the rooftops, seeing nothing. "The fuck?" Simon muttered incredulously.

Cautiously, Mai stepped from behind the dumpster and eyed the carnage. "What was that?" she asked as she wiped her tears away.

"No idea. Come on, let's go," answered Simon, leading the way.

*****

From their cover atop one of the dilapidated, abandoned building rooftops, Kenji and Fiona watched as Simon and Mai ran away. Fiona held an M72 LAWS missile launcher; Kenji's Ruger Super Redhawk was still in his hand.

"I love this thing," said Fiona, cradling the M72 like a mother might hug her child.

"I noticed," Kenji grunted as he slipped his revolver back into his holster.

"You're just sore because you couldn't use your pussy-ass sniper rifle," Fiona replied.

"As I recall, that 'pussy-ass' sniper rifle saved *your* ass on more than one occasion," Kenji retorted with a dry grin.

"Yeah … well," stammered Fiona as she tried to come up with a sufficient comeback. "Man. Fuck you."

"Whatever," muttered Kenji. "I'm calling the boss." Walking away from Fiona, he pressed the button on the communicator of his earpiece. "EYEBALL, this is SNAPPER. We just bailed Kane and Mai out of some shit, over," Kenji said.

"Understood. Did they see you?" asked Ben.

"No, but they're gonna be suspicious," Kenji answered wryly. "Unless they believe in angels."

"Return to HQ ASAP," replied Ben.

"Roger that," Kenji said as he turned to face Fiona.

She'd hoped to overhear things better. "Well?" Fiona asked impatiently.

"He told us to head back home," Kenji answered bluntly.

Fiona made a face and grinned. "Shit, just when things were starting to get interesting!"

Chapter 14

Plan B

Usually the Triad's central control room was quiet, but with the entire island currently ensconced in an all-out war, the room was considerably more hectic than usual. Deng sat in the back room staring at the screen on the wall, furious and frustrated at the news Mazin had just given him.

"How the hell could this have happened?" Deng asked.

"Sir, it was shot down. We believe the pilot is dead," said Mazin as Deng turned around to face him.

Deng slammed his fist on the table in anger. *Not Wei, too.* "Damn! Those Rojas bastards will hang for this," growled Deng. He sighed, quickly regaining his composure.

"What is the status of Simon and Mai?" he asked.

"At the moment we believe they're still alive, but we won't know for sure until we hear from them," Mazin replied.

"We'll assume they're alive, then," Deng said as he picked up his headset. "How is the rest of our little war going?" he asked.

"Excellent. Between our forces and the Russians, all of the Rojas Cartel's territory on Sankan should be under our control within forty-eight hours," Mazin answered.

Deng sighed with a bit less stress, pleased with Mazin's report. "It's good to know *something's* going according to plan," he muttered dryly.

*****

Simon and Mai ran as fast as they could through the decrepit back alleys of Sankan City. Behind them, they still heard Cartel soldiers following them. Simon turned and fired two bullets at them as they ran. They ducked into another alley and finally stopped. As Mai caught her breath, Simon checked to see if there were any more pursuers. Satisfied with what he observed, he shifted his attention to Mai.

"We're safe; they're not following," he said as he holstered his Jericho. He turned to her, only to see Mai's fist coming straight at his face. He caught it with his hand before it hit him. "There a problem?" Simon asked sarcastically, her fist still in his hand.

"You murderous bastard! How could you leave Wei there to die?" asked Mai, her face contorted with rage born of grief.

"*Leave* him,'" Simon repeated. Simon pulled Mai towards him by her fist until their faces were inches from each other, then grabbed her by her shirt collar with his other hand. "Lady, do you think I *wanted* to leave him there to die? There was nothing I could do to save him. How about honoring his memory instead of attacking me?" Simon growled.

He let her go with enough force that she stumbled a little backwards, sitting down hard.

Simon glared down at Mai. "Now, look, you don't like me. I get that. Frankly I don't care why. *However*, I am your best shot at getting the hell off this rock and back to the land of make-believe, so I'd really appreciate less lip!" he admonished sternly.

"What do you mean by the land of make - believe?" Mai asked.

"George Orwell once said that people sleep peacefully in their beds at night because rough men stand ready to do violence on their behalf," Simon replied.

"I'm familiar with the quote," Mai said.

"Yeah? Well, what he's really saying is that if you want peace, you *need* guys like me who are willing to do what needs to be done. So you can keep living in the land of make-believe," Simon explained. "That's my take on it, anyway." He shrugged. "The bad guys won't go away just because you want them to. Every now and them a trigger has to be pulled," Simon continued.

"That's … an interesting interpretation," Mai replied thoughtfully.

"Everything means something to someone," grunted Simon dismissively, tired of the conversation but mostly, just tired. "That guy Wei - what was he to you?" he asked.

"I knew him since I was five. He was one of my father's bodyguards … and my sometime babysitter," answered Mai.

Simon nodded sympathetically. "I'm sorry. If it's any consolation, I know how you feel," said Simon apologetically.

Mai was livid. "How could you possibly know how I feel? You're just a mercenary that thrives on the suffering of others," she cried, brushing herself off as she stood up.

Simon's mood shifted from sympathy back to anger. "Word of advice, lady: Until you've seen what I've seen and done what I've done, don't fucking tell me that I don't know what it's like to lose someone!" he said tersely.

The sudden change of tone took Mai by surprise. She realized by the look in Simon's eye that she had been wrong. "Please forgive me. I shouldn't have … I didn't …," began Mai meekly.

"You sure as hell didn't," Simon interrupted. "Forget it. I'm used to being condemned by people like you." He glanced out of the alley to check for pursuers. When he saw that it was still clear, he leaned back behind cover.

For a few seconds, they were both quiet, unsure of what to say.

"So … what now?" Mai asked finally, desperate to make amends.

"I'm gonna call Deng and find out," answered Simon.

"How?" inquired Mai curiously.

"I guess you didn't notice before. Deng gave me a wireless radio earpiece to contact him," Simon explained. *She sure notices plenty of other things to complain about.* Simon pressed the call button on the earpiece and began speaking. "RED POLE, are you there? This is MONOLITH, over," he said.

For a few seconds, he heard nothing, not even static. He was about to try again when suddenly Deng's voice buzzed over the earpiece.

"MONOLITH? Is LOTUS okay?" Deng asked frantically.

"She's dandy … and so am I, by the way," said Simon dryly.

"Good," said Deng.

"Yeah, so where are we? And what's the plan to get us out of here?" Simon asked impatiently.

"Stand by," said Deng.

Simon could hear Deng barking orders to his men in Mandarin on the other end. Within minutes, Mazin had presented Deng with a small laptop computer on which a live map of the island clearly showed Simon and Mai's location on the screen.

Their location was likely to be a problem. "Damn," grunted Deng, while writing instructions quickly for Mazin, who promptly obeyed.

"That doesn't sound good," muttered Simon.

"The short answer is that you're screwed," replied Deng blatantly.

"What else is new?" asked Simon sarcastically. "The question is how *badly*?"

"Very," answered Deng. "You're knee-deep in Cartel territory. To make matters worse, we can't send in another chopper. All of our helicopters are either damaged or occupied elsewhere."

"Damn. So what the fuck do we do?" Simon asked.

From across the room, Mazin nodded to Deng by way of an answer. Deng nodded back and continued casually, "I've instructed the *Zheng* to come ashore and pick you up." Deng paused. "The bad news is that you will have to fight your way to the harbor to reach it," he said.

"That's on the other side of the city, isn't it?" asked Simon.

"Yes, but Mazin has determined the quickest and safest route to get there and has already sent the directions to your phone," replied Deng.

"Any chance of backup or support?" Simon asked.

"Regrettably, no. All Triad forces are otherwise engaged," answered Deng.

"What about Vasilev? Can the Syndicate help?" asked Simon, thinking of Sasha.

"Again no. They're on the other side of the city attacking Cartel property. I hate to say it, but you and Mai are on your own," Deng replied.

Then who was it that saved us earlier? thought Simon. He decided not to say anything about the incident.

"Good luck," continued Deng before ending the transmission.

"Great," grunted Simon.

Simon pulled out his phone and examined the directions to get to the docks. When he felt Mai behind him, trying to looking over his shoulder, he turned his head. "Something I can help you with?" he asked brusquely.

Mai pointed to the phone. "Are those directions to get out of here?" she inquired.

"Yep, there's a ship waiting for us at the docks. 'Problem is, we're going to have to fight our way through the Cartel's territory to get there," answered Simon.

"I see. How are we going to do that without a car?" said Mai.

"Easy. We steal a car and head straight for the docks," answered Simon nonchalantly as he put the phone in his pocket and pulled out his Jericho 941.

"That doesn't sound so easy," said Mai, unconvinced.

"Nothing ever is," said Simon as he reloaded the gun. "C'mon, we'd better get moving."

Chapter 15

Fatal Interlude

Sasha Molotova looked out the window of the Vasilev Syndicate helicopter as it flew above the city. The view was hellish, awash with the fire of war and the thunderous cacophony of gunfire and explosions. Her mind drifted back to the briefing with Arbanov the night before. Her mission was to assassinate key Cartel members; currently she was en route to kill Raimundo Calzado. According to his file, he was the Rojas Cartel's head of operations on Sankan Island. She had memorized both his face and his file last night.

Arbanov sent her in with five of the Syndicate's best men led by Orb Marius. The plan was simple enough: Orb and his men would storm the gates of the compound via armored car, distracting its defenders while Sasha landed on the roof and killed Calzado.

According to Calzado's file he was hiding in the only mansion on the island, which served as the Cartel's base on Sankan. While Sasha was going after Calzado, a joint task force of Syndicate and Triad commandos would hunt down and assassinate the remaining Cartel elites that were either foolish or unlucky enough to remain on the island. Arbanov was confident that the plan would not only cripple the Cartel permanently in Asia, but also send a message to its leadership in Brazil.

Sasha felt the helicopter tilt sharply to the right, jolting her from her thoughts. *Almost there,* she thought. She lifted her scoped Mauser C96 Broomhandle pistol out of its holster, inserted a fresh magazine and holstered it again. A rifle would have been nice to have along, but also too clumsy for the job.

She looked out the window at the embattled city. Columns of smoke rose all across the city. The muffled staccato of gunshots came from many directions. *I wonder where Simon is in all of that?* thought Sasha.

Sasha turned her head away from the window just as a red light blinked on, signifying her arrival at the multi-storied and ornate mansion. She stood up as straight as space would allow, walked towards the door and opened it to disembark. Outside on the roof, guards scampered about, firing at the chopper. In response, the pilot strafed the roof with the helicopter's mini-gun, killing them.

As the chopper hovered a few feet off the surface, Sasha watched as two Syndicate armored cars crashed through the front gate and men jumped out. The chopper rotors were still spinning as Sasha jumped out onto the roof of the mansion. As soon as she was off, the helicopter rose back up into the sky, turned and flew away to its next task.

Sasha walked to the edge of the roof, stepping over the bodies of the dead guards, looking in all directions as she did. She pulled a small piton gun out of her pack and fired a spike into the roof's edge; a rope was attached to it. She attached the piton gun to a clip on her belt and began slowly rappelling down the side of the mansion, stopping just above a tall window. She pulled a mirror out of her belt and angled it to see if there was anyone on the other side of the window. In the reflection she saw two men yelling at each other. Their backs were to the window, however. Were they armed?

Pushing off of the side, she took care to control her rate of descent before crashing feet first through the window. Her feet slammed into the back of one of the men. The second was shocked, even terrified, at her dramatic entrance. She landed on the first man's back as he lay face down on the floor, moaning in pain.

Sasha pulled out her C96 and shot the man standing in front of her as he reached for his pistol. After holstering the pistol, she turned her attention to the man beneath her. In one swift motion, she stood up, grabbed him by the back of his neck and the seat of his pants and dragged him to the gaping broken window. Expertly leveraging his weight, she held him poised over the sill.

"Where is Calzado?" asked Sasha in Portuguese.

"Fuck you. I'm not telling you anything, bitch. You broke my fucking nose!" replied the man.

"Then you must quickly learn to fly," said Sasha, pretending to throw him out the window.

"Wait, wait! I'll talk," pleaded the man.

"Goooood ...," she said approvingly, waiting for more.

"He's in the panic room on the bottom floor," the man said.

"Excellent," muttered Sasha. Standing him up, she slammed him face first into the wall by the window, knocking him out.

Out of the corner of her eye, Sasha saw the man she had shot rising up behind her, just to her left. Instinctively, she swung around, reached for a throwing knife in her belt and threw it at his stomach. He staggered backwards towards the window and fell out.

"Should have stayed down," muttered Sasha.

Drawing her Mauser, she cocked it and walked cautiously towards the door. Memorizing the mansion's blueprint had passed some time at the Syndicate's HQ; she knew exactly where the panic room was. Sasha opened the door slightly and peeked out, seeing no one.

The door opened onto a balcony overlooking the mansion's opulent entrance hall. It, too, was vacant. To her left and right were stairs leading down to the hall and ultimately, to the front door of the mansion. Beyond the stairs on both sides of the balcony were doors. Hanging from the ceiling was a magnificent crystal chandelier with gold hardware. It glistened in the afternoon sunlight, creating a prismatic rainbow on the walls. The chandelier reminded her of pictures she had seen in a book years ago – pictures of the Winter Palace, when the Czars ruled Russia.

As she approached the left flight of stairs, a door on the right side of the balcony swung open. Two guards stepped out carrying AK-47s, one of which had an under-barrel grenade launcher attached. Their surprise at seeing a beautiful woman quickly faded; they took aim. Before they could pull their triggers, however, she shot one in the head, then the other.

Sasha ran over to their lifeless bodies, holstered her pistol and picked up the AK-47 with the grenade launcher. She slid two magazines into the empty pouches in her belt. *Couldn't hurt.*

Slowly she descended the stairs, her senses primed for another attack. She heard gunfire outside. If she listened closely enough, she could hear Orb barking orders to his men. He was an odious individual, she thought, but he got the job done.

When she reached the bottom of the stairs, Sasha found the locked basement access door and kicked it open. A short flight of stairs put her inside a wine cellar. She would have enjoyed appropriating a few bottles of what she could tell at a glance were expensive brands, but she had neither the room nor the time.

Beyond the wine rack she found a solid steel door with an electronic lock. Slinging the rifle over her shoulder by its strap, she took a moment to study the lock. The door was so thick that although she could hear muffled sounds coming from inside, as if from a great distance, she could not identify them.

Emblazoned on the front of the lock were the words Applied Dynamics. A Rest Easy 500 electronic lock with password identification software – one of the more expensive and secure digital locks available on the market. Ordinarily, it would take hours for Sasha to open the lock, but before accepting this job she had serendipitously purchased a special electronic lock pick from the Guild's lounge in Tokyo.

Sasha pulled the pick out of her small pack; the size of a cell phone, it had two short wires protruding from its back. Plugging the wires into the lock, she pushed the appropriate buttons and held her breath.

Please wait, the screen read, following by three blinking red dots. After 30 seconds, as the display seamlessly changed to *Done*, the lights shone green and the lock clicked open. Sasha returned the pick to her belt and positioned the AK before opening the door.

*****

As Sasha finagled the lock, Calzado was on the other side of the door inside the panic room, yelling desperately into a cellphone.

"Mr. Zero, you Networc people were supposed to protect me! That was the deal!" barked a frustrated Calzado.

"True, Mr. Calzado. However, *you* were supposed to force the Triad off Sankan Island," replied Mr. Zero coldly.

"Please ... I need more time!" begged Calzado, sounding more desperate with each second.

"Time is a luxury we cannot afford. Since you failed to uphold your end of the bargain, I see no reason to uphold ours. Good day to you, sir," said Mr. Zero before hanging up.

Before he could utter another word, Calzado heard the worst sound he could hear, given his circumstances: The door of the panic room clicked open. In walked a beautiful blonde woman with an eye patch over her right eye, wearing a black cat suit and holding an AK-47 aimed directly at his forehead. He immediately recognized her as the Guild assassin codenamed KATYUSHA.

The phone dropped to the floor as Calzado raised his hands in surrender. His mind raced to think of a way to get out of this. *Wasn't there a story about this one ...?*

"*You!* The great KATYUSHA! I know you! Your reputation precedes you!" he gushed manically. "I can pay you! 'Give you whatever you want! I can even give you Intel on … on … *Aquarius*," pleaded Calzado, suddenly remembering the name as her trigger finger twitched slightly.

Sasha's curiosity was piqued. "Aquarius?" she frowned as she spat out the hated name.

Calzado smiled. She was obviously interested. Perhaps he would not die today after all.

"Yes … I have a disc that could lead you to its leader," Calzado said.

"Show me," ordered Sasha.

Calzado knelt down and opened a box of computer discs near him on the floor. He quickly flipped through it until he found one. Standing, he handed it to her before raising his hands again. It did indeed say "Aquarius" on the label.

"I always keep records of the people I do business with," said Calzado with a smug grin.

Sasha slung the AK over her shoulder so that she could hold the disc in her hands, turning ever so slightly away from the man as she inspected it.

When Calzado slowly lowered his arms, Sasha did not object. Convinced that he was safe, Calzado inched backwards to the door as Sasha slipped the disc into her belt. Before he could reach the door, however, Sasha unholstered her pistol, whipped around and fired a single bullet at the back of his neck.

"Thank you," said Sasha dryly. She walked over to his body and took a picture of his body with her phone and emailed it to Arbanov. He would require audio confirmation too. She dialed Arbanov's number. "It's done, I'm heading out," said Sasha before quickly hanging up.

First, though, she returned to the box of discs, flipping through the compartments. There were several more labeled Aquarius, many more, in fact – *The bastard managed to tell the truth and hold out on me at the same time.* She slipped all of them into her pack.

Sasha was walking back up the basement stair to the entrance hall when the building was rocked by a tremendous explosion. She braced herself by grabbing onto the railings next to the stairs then quickly ascended the stairs, her mind still focused on the discs and what they might reveal.

Orb and his men stood triumphantly in the hall. "Well?" asked Orb.

"Calzado is dead," Sasha replied. To the men, she said, "Let's go."

"You heard the lady … move!" yelled Orb as he motioned for them to head out of the building.

Sasha followed them as they raced for the truck that had brought them there. Orb got in the driver's seat and started the engine as Sasha slipped in beside him. This surprised him.

"What?" she asked, seeing the look on his face. "I trust being alone with your men about as much as you trust me," she explained.

"Glad we understand each other," replied Orb as they pulled away from the mansion. "But don't ever, *ever*, give an order to my men again."

Sasha turned her head to look out the window so he wouldn't see her smirk. *Always hit them where it hurts.*

*****

At that moment, several miles away in the mountainous badlands north of the city, unknown to anyone else on the island, a man in a black trench coat, black pants with a gray belt, and a black dress shirt with tie and gloves stood at the ready. Atop his head was a wide-brimmed black fedora with a gray band around it. He was, in fact, an agent for the secret organization most agencies regarded as myth and others, as a conspiracy theory: the Networc.

Known only as Counselor Soames, the man belonged to the Networc's elite covert operations branch known as the Upper Echelon. He had been dispatched to Sankan Island to observe the conflict, given control of an unmanned drone orbiting the island several thousand feet above the island. The drone carried a lone AGM-114 Hellfire missile that was trained on Calzado's mansion.

Calzado was dead. Various hidden surveillance equipment in the mansion had verified it all, and it was time to destroy any trace of the Networc's involvement in this conflict. He pulled a small remote out of his coat pocket and pressed a button on it.

"A shame it had to come to this, but ... ashes to ashes, as they say," muttered Counselor Soames.

Instantly a missile jettisoned forth from the drone, rushing towards the island while the drone sped away from it. Counselor Soames returned the remote to his pocket as a car pulled up behind him. Two commandos of the Networc's Lower Echelon had been dispatched to the island to take him to the extraction point. Counselor Soames got in the car and they drove off.

*****

Sasha turned in her seat to take one last glimpse of the mansion as the truck drove away. Something – *Is that a –?* – seemed to fall out of the clouds above. Whatever it was, it was heading straight for the mansion.

"Oh, shit!" yelled Sasha in horror as she realized what it was.

"What?!" Orb exclaimed, startled by her outburst.

"Just DRIVE …," said Sasha frantically as the mansion exploded violently in a blinding fireball of sound and fury. When the smoke cleared, she knew that all that would be left was rubble.

The shock wave and cloud of debris from the blast engulfed the Russian vehicles. Instinctively, Sasha grabbed onto her seat as Orb tried to stabilize the truck. When the explosion ended, Sasha, Orb and the other men were elated, genuinely surprised that they had survived the blast.

Orb stopped the truck. Everyone got out to stare at the cloud of smoke rising from the ruins of the once opulent mansion, still dumbfounded.

"What the hell was that?" asked Orb.

"I don't know, but I'll bet we both have a pretty good idea who does," said Sasha.

Orb nodded grimly as they got back in the truck and headed for the Syndicate's HQ.

*****

Thousands of miles away in Switzerland, in the CEO's office of Kronos International, sat the leader of the Networc. Known to his subordinates only as Mr. Zero, he sat at his desk analyzing his computer screen. In the center of the screen was a live video feed via satellite of Calzado's mansion – or rather, what was left of it. The words: TARGET DESTROYED suddenly flashed on screen in bright red letters.

Mr. Zero grinned in satisfaction. A window on the left of the screen listed the drone's current location: currently over the ocean, heading away from Sankan. With the mouse, he moved the cursor to a button under the GPS that read SELF-DESTRUCT and clicked on it.

The screen went black as, thousands of miles away, the drone exploded, its wreckage falling into the ocean, never to be seen again.

"Like a broom to our footprints," muttered Mr. Zero.

Chapter 16

Reverberations

Underneath the Triad's building in the control room, a technician handed a radar report to Mazin. He read it, then reread it. Mazin looked at the technician skeptically.

"Is this for real?" asked Mazin. The technician nodded.

Mazin motioned for the tech to return to his post. Shaking his head, Mazin went to Deng's office in the back of the control room and showed the report to his superior.

Deng read carefully before letting out a long sigh. "Let me get this straight – an unidentified drone fired a missile at Calzado's mansion?" he asked Mazin.

"Yes, sir. Could ... it be the Americans?" Mazin suggested.

It was a legitimate question. The greatest fear of Sankan's criminal leaders was that certain nations – the U.S. included – would invade the island, resulting in a battle the organizations could not win.

Deng stood up and looked out at the control room. "It's not the Americans. And it sure as hell wasn't our former government either. I know exactly who fired that missile: It was the Networc," Deng answered.

"How do you know, sir?" asked Mazin, confused.

"Simple deduction. We've long suspected that the Networc was in league with the Cartel here. Now that the Cartel is losing, they've obviously decided to tie up any loose ends," said Deng.

"But why not just bomb us instead?" Mazin asked.

"They wouldn't use a drone to kill us; they'd send in one of their assassins to do it personally. Besides, those arrogant bastards in the Networc would make sure we knew it was them coming after us," answered Deng.

They were both silent for a few seconds, mulling. "What if it's the Russians?" asked Mazin.

Their treaty with the Russians was tenuous at best. It kept them from killing each other, but neither trusted the other, and both knew it. The treaty was merely an attempt to prevent a war that risked destroying them both.

Deng shook his head. "It's not them. If they were going to breach the treaty they would have done it sooner," he said, pulling out his cellphone. "Besides, not even the Russians are that crazy." Dialing Pavel Arbanov's number, he continued. "Still, it won't hurt to be sure."

After a few rings Pavel answered with a gruff, "Yes?"

"Deng here. Do you know anything about that blast?" Deng asked, careful with his words lest he insult Pavel or anyone else listening in.

"No! It almost killed some of my men. Luckily they got out just in time. Do *you* know anything about it?" answered Pavel.

"My best guess is that it was a drone strike by an unknown party – but I believe it was fired by the Networc," Deng said.

On the other end of the conversation, Pavel rolled his eyes – a common occurrence when the Networc was mentioned. "I don't have time for conspiracy theories. Let me know when you have something important to tell me." Pavel hung up without the usual pleasantries.

"What did he say?" Mazin asked.

"He knew nothing about it," answered Deng.

"What about Simon, sir?" asked Mazin. "And Mai?"

"Yes, of course. That is the immediate issue. Perhaps it's time we called the Flying Fish and asked for a pickup," said Deng as he tapped on Ben Martin's name in his list of contacts.

*****

At Sankan harbor, in the headquarters of the Flying Fish Trading Company, a similar scene was playing out. Ben Martin sat in front of his computer screen surveying the ruins of

Calzado's mansion via satellite. Kenji Yamada aka SNAPPER, and Fiona Ramos, aka BARRACUDA, stood behind him, keeping the assessment lively.

"Definitely a drone," said Kenji.

"Thanks, Captain Obvious," commented Fiona sarcastically.

"The real question is who fired it," replied Ben. "Obviously it wasn't American or we'd have been notified. It wasn't the Triad. Not the Syndicate. No other country is currently in the mix," he reasoned.

Ben pointed to a little flash on the screen. "And according to thiiiiis," he said, "the drone just blew up over the ocean after it left Sankan Island."

"Hey, look at that!" said Fiona, reaching around Ben to point to another section of the screen. Near the mansion, a truck was driving away from the wreckage.

"That's definitely the Russians," said Kenji dismissively.

"It's always the fucking Russians," Fiona quipped.

"So what now, boss?" asked Kenji. Both he and Fiona lived for action.

Ben swung the chair around and looked up at them. "This changes things considerably," he said.

"What about Simon? Where is he?" asked Kenji.

Ben glanced at another monitor, locked onto Simon Kane. "According to this, he's near Sario Boulevard," he answered.

"Shouldn't we help him? Sario's crawling with Cartel scum," Kenji said.

Ben shook his head. "First we call NARRATOR for authorization. In the meantime, Simon can handle himself till we have orders," answered Ben. As if in response, his cellphone rang.

"Talk about timing," Ben said as the screen lit up. "That's NARRATOR now." He put the call on speaker.

"Hello, sir; you're on speaker. SNAPPER and BARRACUDA and I were just talking about you," said Ben.

"We're aware of the drone strike on the Cartel mansion. What's MONOLITH's current status?" Connors asked from across the world.

"Alive for now," answered Ben.

"Yo, NARRATOR," Fiona interrupted. "Do you know who sent that drone?" she asked.

"Not at this time," answered Connors.

"Sir, it's getting fierce here. I recommend we either backup MONOLITH or bug out," said Ben.

Connors thought for a few seconds. If they intervened, it might blow their cover, not to mention potentially costing Silhouette several good agents. Conversely, if they didn't, and *Simon* was killed, they lost their best – probably their *only* – chance of finding the Networc. The first option was grim; the second, unacceptable.

"EYEBALL, you and your team resume covert assistance. Do not, I repeat, do not make contact with him unless his life is in danger," instructed Connors.

"Yes sir, we'll handle it," Ben replied.

"Good luck," offered Connors before hanging up.

Ben laid his phone on the desk. "Well, guys, you heard him," he said.

Fiona smiled as she rubbed her hands together. "Finally! Some action!" she said excitedly.

"Not for you, though," answered Ben.

Fiona put her hands on her slender hips. "The fuck?" she demanded, annoyed.

"Here's the plan. *Kenji,*" Ben began, ignoring Fiona, "I'm sending you out. Grab a sniper rifle and the Uzi those Cambodians sold us the other day. Take the motorcycle and follow Simon – you can track him from the phone. But remember – no direct interference, got it?" he ordered.

Kenji nodded and walked to the armory to get ready.

"What about me?" asked Fiona.

"You stay with me. Kenji's more suited for stealth work than you are," Ben explained.

"Yeah, 'cause I'm not a bitch," muttered Fiona.

"You sure about that?" yelled Kenji from the armory. He was known for his keen hearing.

"You want to die, motherfucker?!" Fiona yelled.

"Not today," Kenji yelled back.

Fiona shrugged and walked briskly outside to work on the *Rumrunner*.

As Ben watched her storm off, he realized that their orders might arouse the ire of the Triad. A phone call interrupted his thoughts. A glance at the caller ID made him whistle in surprise. For the second time in a few minutes, it was as if his phone could read his mind.

"What's up, Deng?" asked Ben.

"Mr. Martin," Deng began formally. "We have a package we'd like you to escort for us, an American man with an eye patch and a Chinese woman. They're traveling to a ship of ours called the *Zheng* at the docks, and we think they need help," Deng explained.

"Is this the same guy I saw on your roof the other day?" asked Ben. No need to give the impression he knew exactly who Deng meant.

"Yes. A good observation as always, Ben. Once they are on board we want you to act as security while the ship takes them to Taiwan." Deng paused. "The Triad cannot overemphasize the importance of their safety. If any harm comes to the package, indescribable pain will come to you and your team," he said threateningly.

Ben and the rest of Task Force 666 had been on the island long enough to know that a threat from Deng was worth considering, but there was still the matter of their fee.

"Uh-huh. Well, our fee for a spur-of-the-moment job like this is ... fifteen thousand," replied Ben. *Even though it was already our orders, sort of. No reason we can't make a little money off of them.*

"Understood. You will be paid when the ship arrives in Taiwan," said Deng.

"Consider it done," answered Ben.

"We will *consider* it done when it *is* done, Mr. Martin. We will, of course, arrange for your return back to Sankan Island," replied Deng before hanging up.

"Helluva coincidence," Ben muttered as he slipped the phone into his pocket. He walked into the armory. Kenji was making final preparations, armed to the teeth with an Uzi, China Lake grenade launcher and his weapon of choice: a Knight's Armament SR-25 sniper rifle.

"Change of plans, Kenji. Fiona and I will meet you at the *Zheng*, then we're headed for Taiwan," said Ben. As part of their surveillance, they kept constant tabs on where all Triad, Syndicate, and Cartel ships and planes happened to be at any given time on Sankan.

"Got it," replied Kenji, securing a few more small items onto his belt.

He walked outside to relay the change of plans to Fiona. *She'll be happy, no doubt.* He found her working on the plane's engine.

"Sup, boss?" asked Fiona.

"New gig. Get ready, then get in the jeep. We're going to the *Zheng*," Ben replied.

Fiona was confused as she wiped her greasy hands on a rag. "Why?" she asked.

"The Triad wants us to escort Simon to the *Zheng* and ultimately to Taiwan. Kenji will escort Simon and the girl there. You and I will rendezvous at the *Zheng*," explained Ben.

Fiona grinned with excitement. That scenario included at least the possibility of a fight. "I'll go get Bart and Lisa," she replied.

Throwing down the rag, she trotted into the armory and grabbed some magazines, then pulled out her double vertical shoulder holster. She inserted her twin Smith & Wesson 645 pistols, fondly dubbed Bart and Lisa, loaded them with fresh magazines, then joined Ben outside.

Ben already had the engine running.

Fiona climbed enthusiastically into the jeep, slapping the side of the vehicle. "Let's rock it!"

Chapter 17

In Destruction's Shadow

"What the fuck was that?" exclaimed Simon when they heard a violent explosion behind them in the distance.

Simon and Mai were navigating the labyrinthine back alleys of Sankan City to avoid Cartel patrols. The explosion stopped them in their tracks. A tower of black smoke rose above the outline of trees and buildings at some distance.

"What happened?" Mai asked, echoing Simon's surprise.

"I'm guessing *someone* had a bad day," said Simon sarcastically.

"Was it a bomb?" suggested Mai.

Simon had some ideas, but thought it best to avoid such details. "I think we have bigger things to worry about," said Simon, walking briskly away. "We need to keep moving."

Mai complied, but whispered loudly as she jogged to catch up with him. "A mysterious explosion isn't something to worry about?" she hissed.

"Tell you what – why don't you worry about that, and I'll worry about getting our asses out of here alive," replied Simon.

As he said the words, he heard other men talking not far from them. Simon grabbed Mai roughly, pulling her behind the nearest corner for cover. Before Mai could speak, Simon put his hand over her mouth and motioned with his other hand to her that danger was just around the bend.

With Mai suitably settled and quiet, Simon peered out. Across from their alleyway was a small parking lot, in the middle of which sat a covered military transport truck. Four armed Cartel soldiers were loading crates into the truck. Simon smiled.

"That truck is our ticket out of here," whispered Simon as he removed his hand from her mouth.

"What are you going to do?" Mai asked.

"Ask them nicely to let me borrow it," Simon said snidely. "What do you *think* I'm going to do? Stay here," he ordered.

Simon waited until the men's backs were to him, then he ran out, taking cover behind a stack of crates. When the coast was clear, he ran to the front of the truck and slowly inched his way to the other side, staying as close to the ground as he could.

He'd seen a tell-tale wisp of smoke – the driver was having a smoke by the truck. Now Simon saw that the driver's belt holster held a Glock. He flicked his left wrist back; the blade popped out of the armband.

The driver was lost in thought, conveniently turned the other way. When Simon inched close enough, he stood and casually tapped the man on the shoulder. When he turned around, the cigarette fell from his mouth as he started to shout. Simon stabbed him in the stomach before he could make a sound, grabbed him by his shirt collar and slammed his head onto the hood of the truck.

At the noise, the other three Cartel men ran over with their guns cocked, yelling at Simon in Portuguese. Simon held the driver's limp body in front of him as a shield, one arm wrapped tightly around the man's neck. As the gunmen took aim, Simon pulled the Glock out of the driver's holster with his other hand and shot them.

Tossing both body and Glock to the ground, Simon jumped up into the cab of the truck. Fortunately the keys were still in the ignition. As the engine roared to life, Simon tapped the knife back into the armband on the dashboard.

Simon backed the truck up to the alley, where Mai was waiting obediently. He opened his door. "Get in!" he barked as he scooted over to the passenger seat.

Mai quickly ran out to the truck and stopped at the door. "I'm not –"

"You *are*. Driving," said Simon casually.

"I've never driven a truck," protested Mai.

"First time for everything," Simon replied.

Arguing with the man would be futile, especially in their current situation. Mai sighed and pulled herself up into the truck. She stepped on the gas, and the truck lurched forward in gratifying cooperation.

Simon gestured to the left with his thumb and Mai turned the wheel, eyeing him for further instructions. When there were none, she sped up, now on a main street.

The city streets were virtually empty. Occasionally they'd see what looked like people running in the shadows between the buildings. *It won't be long now,* mused Simon anxiously as they drove onward.

Suddenly the truck slowed to a stop at a four-way intersection.

"Why are you stopping?" asked Simon surprised. He whipped his head in all directions, on the alert for attack. Nothing.

"They have the right of way," Mai explained, nodding to the right.

"Seriously?" replied Simon. "You're following fucking driving etiquette?!"

She pointed to four motorcycles approaching. Simon squinted. It was too dark to identify them. The bikers slowed as well.

Simon studied them cautiously. They might be Triads coming to their rescue ... but he and Mai were inside an enemy truck. "Wait a minute ..."

The bikers recognized them. They pulled out guns, mostly pistols and Uzi submachine guns.

"Oh, shit! Go now!" Simon yelled.

Mai slammed her foot on the gas and they jumped forward as the bikers revved their engines.

"Keep going, I'll worry about them," shouted Simon, eyeing the side mirror.

All four bikers were now following in hot pursuit.

"Well?" Mai cried as a fusillade of bullets hit the back of the truck.

"That answer your question?" Simon said harshly.

"What do we do now?" Mai's voice was panicked, but she drove on.

"Don't worry. Me and Mr. Jericho will take care of it," said Simon as he drew his pistol.

Simon leaned out the window and fired three quick shots at them. Instinctively, the bikers moved behind the truck.

"Now stop. Mai!" Simon yelled.

Mai hit the brakes and the truck squealed to a stop. Almost instantaneously they heard the impact of four objects crashing into the rear.

"Now go!" barked Simon.

Mai stepped on the gas while Simon looked out the window behind them. The bikers lay scattered and still, some of the tires of the motorcycles still spinning impotently.

Simon gave a little chuckle of triumph as he turned back to Mai.

Mai glanced at him with a disapproving but curious look.

"What?" asked Simon.

Before she could answer, another motorcycle appeared in front of them, still at some distance, followed by a pickup truck with a mounted machine gun in the bed.

"You gotta be fucking kidding me," muttered Simon.

The driver of the motorcycle raised his Uzi at them.

"Get down," yelled Simon just before a barrage of bullets sprayed the windshield, shattering it.

After the opening salvo Simon looked at Mai, who had instinctively braked. "You okay?" asked Simon.

"Yes," Mai answered, adjusting her glasses. Oddly enough, the spray of windshield shards had not injured either of them.

"Good. They sure as hell won't be," said Simon as he aimed the Jericho. Motorcycle or truck? *Truck ...*

He fired two shots at the driver. The first round missed, but the second hit him in the head, killing him instantly. The driver-less truck, now literally out of control, careened towards them.

Mai made a hard left and floored it to avoid a collision. The truck sped past them and violently flipped over, exploding on impact. Before Simon could congratulate Mai for her quick thinking, the motorcycle came out of nowhere behind them and fired another barrage.

"Damn," grunted Simon in annoyance.

Simon leaned out from the window and was about to fire when he suddenly realized that he was out of ammo.

"Ah, fuck," Simon muttered as he narrowly avoided getting shot before ducking his head inside.

The motorcyclist was coming around her side. "Do something!" Mai yelled as bullets bounced off the truck.

"Yes, your majesty," said Simon sarcastically, throwing the Jericho on the seat as he pulled the .38 revolver out of the ankle holster.

"How many guns do you have?" Mai asked, frantic as she drove.

"Enough, I hope," replied Simon dryly. He pushed Mai forward onto the steering wheel as he leaned behind her, pulling back the pistol's hammer.

He waited until the motorcycle was closer, then leaned out the driver's side window and fired one shot at its front tire and another at the biker's chest. Then he quickly hopped back to the passenger side, returning the revolver to his ankle holster. He slid a fresh magazine into the Jericho and leaned his head back, suddenly tired.

"Anyone else following us?" asked Simon as he returned the Jericho to his holster.

"No," Mai answered.

Simon could tell that there was something on her mind and would have asked her about it when suddenly the truck rapidly slowed down.

"I'm not doing anything!" Mai cried as a cloud of smoke erupted from the engine with a loud hiss. Mai tried to maintain control, but the unresponsive power steering made it difficult. "The bullets must have wrecked the engine," she said.

Always something, thought Simon. "Stop the truck. We're gonna have to walk," he said.

Mai pressed hard on the brake and steered as far over as she could. As they got out of the truck, it suddenly occurred to Simon that it was darker outside. There were no streetlights in this part of town, and the crescent moon did little to help. The mission was to have been completed by twenty-one hundred hours. Now approaching that, the end was nowhere in sight.

"We need to find a place to hunker down for the night," said Simon.

"That sounds good, but where?" asked Mai.

Simon looked around, asking himself that very question. Near the edge of the city, they stood on a sidewalk in front of a row of buildings. He drew his Jericho as he kicked open the door of the nearest building.

"After you, mademoiselle," said Simon sarcastically.

Mai shrugged and walked inside, ignoring his rancor. He followed close behind.

They saw no one, heard no one. *Odd. It isn't that old, or in disrepair,* thought Simon. Maybe its inhabitants were just cowering in fear.

Simon and Mai walked up a flight of stairs and down a hallway. At the end of the hall was a wooden door. Simon edged around her and held out his hand. "Wait," he ordered quietly.

Mai waited. Simon approached the door with his gun drawn, and kicked it open. The room was empty, but relatively clean. It was small with one window, furnished with a table and chair, lamp and sofa. As he checked it out, he found a bathroom behind a door on the right wall, then motioned from the hall opening for Mai to come in.

Mai looked around. "Pretty empty," she noticed.

"Yep, that's the Hotel Sankan for you, neither class or ass," Simon quipped.

"Kind of like you," said Mai slyly.

"So you *do* have a sense of humor," said Simon. "Surprise, surprise."

Mai smiled at the joke as she lay down on the couch. Simon sat at the table and put his Jericho on the table. In the growing darkness he saw Mai shift her position just once before her slow, measured breathing told him she was already asleep.

Chapter 18

The Eyeball and the Barracuda

Ben and Fiona, meanwhile, were route to the *Zheng*, located on the other side of Sankan harbor. The harbor had long ago been dubbed the "Devil's Maw" by the island's residents due to its shape and the illicit nature of the cargo that came and went.

"Think we'll see any action?" Fiona asked.

"Probably not," Ben grunted.

"Damn! So … it's just a simple escort job then?" Fiona inquired.

He nodded. "There's no such thing as routine in this line of work, though," Ben added.

"*Hell* yeah! That's why I l love this job," replied Fiona.

Ben knew she meant it. In the two years since the Goon Squad was formed, he had become well-acquainted with his two teammates. Reading Fiona's file initially, he'd been surprised that Connors would enlist someone with her unhinged nature.

When he questioned Connors, he'd been reassured. "You can handle her," Connors had told him. "Her bloodthirsty temperament made her one of the most feared criminals in the Miami underworld. So she's perfect for the Goon Squad," he had explained.

Kenji, on the other hand, was quiet, reserved, collected – like most snipers. Ben recalled Connors saying that the personalities of Kenji and Ben would keep Fiona in check. So far, it had been an accurate assessment.

An unintentional side benefit of Fiona's ruthless nature was that she, and by extension Flying Fish, had earned a reputation for recklessness and borderline insanity on the island. However, she and Flying Fish had also earned a reputation for reliability. They were the first choice for transporting goods for the Triad and Syndicate.

Occasionally Silhouette would task them with a mission in the area. "If field agents like Simon Kane are, or in his case *were*, Silhouette's scalpel, then the Goon Squad is Silhouette's sledgehammer," Connors had said.

This was not a night for reminiscing, however. As they approached the ship, they heard what sounded like gunshots.

"That doesn't sound good," said Ben dryly.

"I disagree," replied Fiona, a smile growing on her face.

As they got closer to the water, they saw three trucks parked next to the ship with seven gunmen behind each. Triad gunners on the ship's deck were keeping them at bay, but they couldn't hold them off forever.

There were four gunmen behind the truck on the right and three on the left. Ben stopped the jeep and pulled out his Desert Eagle, pulling back the slide to cock it.

"Fiona, introduce them to Bart and Lisa," ordered Ben quietly.

"About fucking time!" exclaimed Fiona as she drew her twin 645's.

The two of them jumped out of the jeep. Fiona charged straight at the group of four men. They turned around to face her just as she aimed both pistols at two of them, killing them both. The remaining two men aimed their rifles at her but she kicked one of them in the face, knocking him down. Ben shot the other as he ran towards the three gunmen behind the left truck.

Ben pistol-whipped one of the gunmen in the face and shot the other. The third man ran up behind Ben and pinned him against the truck, causing him to drop his pistol. The two men grappled shortly but Ben's imposing size and strength allowed him to overpower the gunman. Ben punched him repeatedly in the face before smashing his face into the vehicle's window.

While Ben was otherwise engaged, the recipient of Fiona's roundhouse recovered enough to charge her. She jumped onto the man's back, riding him like a stallion. He successfully threw her off, but she still held onto him. Unable to get off a shot because of Fiona's ferocity, he reached back with a blow to her face.

Fiona lept off smoothly and glared at him as a thin strip of blood poured from the cut on her lip. "Okay *puta,* that's how you want to do this?" said Fiona threateningly.

She flipped the pistol in her left hand around and lunged for the man, pistol-whipping him repeatedly in his face with it before shooting him three times in the stomach with the pistol in her right hand.

As Ben dispensed with the man at the truck window, the first man he had put down began to rise unsteadily from the ground, reaching for his weapon. No sooner had Fiona's attacker dropped to the ground than she flipped the pistol back around and fired two shots with both pistols at the man's back, killing him as he aimed at Ben.

It had happened so quickly, Fiona and Ben just stood there for a moment, surveying the carnage around them, finally able to catch their breath.

Fiona held her pistols up, twirled them around her fingers effortlessly before blowing the smoke off of them. "Getting sloppy boss," said Fiona, twirling her pistols a little before she holstered them.

Ben shook his head. "You call this sloppy?" he asked sarcastically as he pointed to the bodies of the men he had dispatched. "This is what I call a team effort. I've had your back plenty of times. 'About time you had mine."

"Whatever, man. I'm just pissed there weren't more of 'em," replied Fiona dejectedly.

"Don't worry, you'll have more opportunities later," a voice called from behind them.

They whipped around, ready to draw their weapons, but relaxed immediately.

"Hey, Chen," said Ben. "Aren't you a sight to behold?"

The captain of the *Zheng* and his men casually walked down the gangplank, flanked by Triad commandos armed with AK−47s, their eyes locked on Fiona.

"How's it going?" asked Ben as he walked up to Chen and held out his hand to shake.

"Better now that you're here! Those bastards appeared out of nowhere," replied Chen.

"Tell your boys to quit staring at me or they'll be *joining* the bastards," growled Fiona, reaching for Bart and Lisa.

When Ben scowled at her she let go of the guns, rolled her eyes and crossed her arms. In response, Chen nodded at his men; they immediately stepped back.

"Deng told you the plan then?" Chen asked.

They both nodded. "Yeah ... we escort them off the island and back to civilization," said Fiona with a grunt.

Chen gave a little bow. "You should know there's been a change," he said.

"What kind of change?" Ben asked, already expecting to not like the answer. He liked to stick with the plan. Still in moments when the plan went awry, he resorted to the slogan he learned while in the United State Marine Corps: Improvise. Adapt. Overcome.

"Perhaps we should continue this in my office," said Chen.

"Lead on," said Ben dryly, preparing for bad news.

Ben and Fiona followed Chen up the gangplank to the ship, through winding corridors and eventually to Chen's office in the stern. Chen sat down behind his desk while Ben and Fiona sat in two separate chairs that faced him.

"Well?" asked Fiona, anxious to get on with things.

"A half hour ago, Deng informed me that he has received a message from the Mountain Master instructing him to personally deliver a message to Simon once the package is on board. We will leave for Taiwan then Deng, Simon and the package will fly to our HQ in Hong Kong," answered Chen.

"That's the plan as we know it," said Ben.

Chen held up a finger to silence him. "However, there's been a slight change," he continued.

"What kind of change?" Ben asked as Fiona rolled her eyes.

"Deng and a Russian agent, codename: KATYUSHA, will be joining us en route to Taiwan," Chen explained.

That is *a surprise,* thought Ben.

"KATYUSHA ? Who is this person?" Fiona asked.

"A Guild assassin. Deng hired her for extra security since she has completed her mission for the Syndicate. As we speak she is en route to this location via helicopter from our building," said Chen.

"And what about this package Simon's escorting?" Ben asked, as if he did not know.

"The identity and nature of the package is highly classified," answered Chen cryptically.

"Of course it fucking is," muttered Fiona as she rolled her eyes.

"Why Taiwan, by the way? Why not go straight to Hong Kong instead?" Ben inquired.

"Taiwan is closer than Hong Kong, plus we don't feel comfortable letting mercenaries into our main headquarters. No offense intended," said Chen.

"None taken," said Ben dismissively.

There was a bit of awkward silence, replaced by the sound of an approaching helicopter.

Chen stood. "Ah, that should be KATYUSHA now. Feel free to follow me to the helipad," he offered.

The helipad was at the bow of the ship. By the time they reached it, the Chinese helicopter had already settled on the pad and the rotors were slowing to a stop. The skin of the chopper was riddled with bullet holes and dents.

As Chen, Ben and Fiona approached, the door slid open revealing a tall and athletic, extremely attractive blonde in a form-fitting black bodysuit. The red accessories and black gloves added to the air of mystery about her, as did the eye patch over her right eye. After closing the door behind her, she walked over to the little welcoming party as the helicopter took off again.

"KATYUSHA, I presume?" asked Ben loudly, to be heard over the chopper's engine.

Ben already knew who she was, of course. He had studied Silhouette's files on the Guild's most high profile member's years ago. He couldn't arouse suspicion about the Flying Fish, however. The less the Triad knew, the better.

"Call me Sasha," replied the woman as they shook hands.

Sasha looked this way and that, surprised that Simon hadn't been there to greet her. She was alarmed by his absence, but hid her concern. "Are Simon and the package below deck?"

"They're not here yet," answered Chen bluntly. "They've taken refuge for the night, but we can expect them some time tomorrow."

Sasha nodded. Although she would never admit it, she was glad to hear that he was still alive.

"What does it matter to you, Catwoman?" Fiona inquired brusquely. "You're just along for the ride, right?

Sasha gazed toward the embattled city, finally quiet for the night, she hoped, then back at Fiona. She could tell Fiona was sizing her up. "Simon is an old ... acquaintance of mine," she said. She stepped toward her and stared her down. "And incidentally, I am not a cat woman."

"I can see that. In that getup, Russkie, you're more like a rejected Bond girl," Fiona retorted smugly, not backing down one iota.

"And you look like you belong in prison," Sasha said.

Fiona stepped closer until her face was mere inches from Sasha's, her fists clenched ready for a fight. "Is that a fact?" growled Fiona.

"If the prison uniform fits," said Sasha with a smirk, clearly unintimidated.

Ben and Chen watched, enjoying the spectacle. It was like having front row seats to a boxing match.

"Ladies, please? Let's not do this, okay?" said Chen, about to step between them.

Ben placed his hand on Chen's shoulder, stopping him. "I wouldn't get in the middle of this, if I were you," he warned.

For a few seconds Fiona and Sasha stood immobile, silent as statues, staring each other down with fists clenched waiting to see who would throw the first blow.

"Ten bucks on Fiona," Ben offered quietly.

Chen shrugged. "Fuck it, I'll put eight on Sasha," he muttered.

Fiona broke the silence with a taunt. "Go ahead, I ain't got all night … Catwoman," she snarled.

In answer, Sasha smiled and unclenched her fists. "I don't deal with mad dogs," she said as she calmly walked past Fiona to her promised quarters.

Taken by surprise, Fiona just stood there trying to think of a comeback to call out, coming up short. She relaxed with a deep sigh. "Damn. I was already for a fight, too," she muttered in disappointment.

"What else is new?" said Ben.

Ben and Fiona shared a knowing glance as they turned to look back at the city. Under cover of darkness, things were quiet for the moment. What would tomorrow bring?

Chapter 19

Angel of Mercy/Angel of Death

It was still dark when Mai woke up to see Simon sitting at the table. The purple sky through the window promised a sunrise fairly soon. He had taken his trench coat off and hung it on the back of the chair. During the night of keeping watch, Simon had meticulously cleaned the wrist knife and the .38. The pistol was securely holstered back on his leg. He was still working on the Jericho; it lay on the table in pieces.

"Sleep well?" Simon asked looking up from his task as she stirred.

"Yes ... despite my current situation," Mai answered.

"Can't have everything," muttered Simon dryly. Even as he spoke, he decided to say something he should have said several hours earlier.

"Listen … what I said earlier. I realize I may have been a little hard on you. For what it's worth, I'm sorry," said Simon softly, continuing to work.

Mai was surprised, but pleased. "It's alright. We did sort of get off on the wrong foot," she joked.

"Yeah, well, shit happens," responded Simon.

Mai straightened her back a little, stretching after the hours of sleeping on a hard couch. *But Simon hasn't slept at all.* "I should apologize too," said Mai.

"Oh?" Simon asked.

"I automatically assumed you were just some brain dead, kill-crazy mercenary." Mai shrugged. "Clearly you are smarter than that, and for that assumption, I apologize," she explained.

"Yeah, believe it or not, I was a triple history, literature and political science major in college," Simon commented as he absentmindedly fingered his cleaning rag.

"Impressive," observed Mai.

"I have my moments," Simon grunted.

Simon noticed that she wore the same curious look on her face he'd noticed the day before as she shifted her gaze to the weapons on the table.

"Something on your mind?" he asked.

"Just a question," Mai asked, suddenly nervous.

"Shoot, we've got plenty of time," responded Simon. He shifted his weight in the chair to face her head-on.

Mai paused, thinking about how to properly word the question she had toyed with in her thoughts. Simon watched the mental gears turning.

"How do you cope ... with killing all those people?" Mai asked finally.

Simon glanced at the objects on the table which had shed so much blood ... and had saved many lives. "I try not to think about it, though I find a sense of humor helps," he answered calmly.

"But ... doesn't it take a toll on you? Psychologically? Emotionally?" Mai asked.

"Probably," Simon said with a shrug.

"Then why do it at all? Why *live* this kind of life?" Mai asked earnestly.

"I wanted to do some good in the world. And if I'm perfectly honest I wanted a ... challenge after college," answered Simon.

"What about the men you've killed, though? Do you feel any sympathy for them?" Mai asked. She stretched her neck back and forth, then stopped. "I don't mean to intrude. But I really want to know," she said quietly.

Simon sighed and leaned back in the chair, suddenly wishing for a drink. He brushed the thought aside. "I suppose that's what it all comes down to, doesn't it? The ability to feel sympathy – isn't that the difference between the good guys and the bad guys? But to answer your question, no," explained Simon. "I do not sympathize with them."

He closed his eye and then turned his attention back to her. "Mai, even when I was in the SEALs ... and then with the agency ... everyone I killed either deserved it or was killed in self -defense," Simon continued, careful not to mention Silhouette by name. "The truth is, we all choose the paths our lives will take. The people I've killed made their choices; I made mine. Put it this way – a friend of mine once said 'whatever will be, will be,'" remembering one of Sheila's favorite sayings.

Having been raised by a former spymaster, Mai knew who he meant by "the agency." "But you don't work for them anymore. Why continue?" Mai asked.

Simon's silence, and the look on his face, told the tale. "You lost someone special, didn't you?" she probed gently.

The memory of Sheila morphed into a vision of her death. "Yes, I did. Just three months ago. The only woman I ever loved was shot in front of me," Simon replied.

Though he tried to hide it, Mai could hear the pain of loss in his voice. "I understand a little of how you feel. I lost my mother when I was young," said Mai, remembering the sound and awful sight as the explosion engulfed the store her mother was in. "Not the loss of a … true love … but there's one thing I still don't understand. How did you come to be *here*, rescuing me?" she asked.

Simon stood and walked aimlessly around the little room. "Your father said he'd help me find the organization responsible for killing her. In exchange for rescuing you," he answered dryly.

Mai dropped her head. "So you're doing all of this for revenge?" she asked.

"No, for *justice*. And before you start, I've already gotten the whole 'revenge isn't justice' speech," Simon replied, "so save your breath. Sometimes the only justice is the justice you make for yourself," he continued.

Mai began walking around the room also, talking almost to herself. "Okay, but what would *she* think of what you're doing?" she asked.

Simon stopped, quiet as he thought of how to respond in a way Mai could comprehend.

"She'd understand," he said finally. "Everyone deserves justice. It is the only thing, the *last* thing, I can do for her. To make sure she didn't die for nothing," Simon continued softly.

Mai stopped where she was, right in front of him. "I see. What was her name?" she asked, looking directly up at him.

Simon was puzzled. "What?" he asked.

"The woman you lost – what was her name?" clarified Mai.

"Why do you want to know?" Simon responded.

"I'm naturally curious. And besides, since I'm playing a part in your revenge, don't I have a right to know?" asked Mai.

Before Simon could respond, the door was suddenly kicked open. Two Asian men with unnaturally large smiles stood in the doorway, their black hair long and greasy. One of them was large, muscular and bearded, twice Simon's size. The other was shorter and rat-faced, his shining eyes locked on Mai. The scars on the sides of their mouths told Simon exactly who they were.

Smiling Boys. Deng's photo had not done their creepiness justice. "Sorry guys, room's taken. Get your own," said Simon, ready for a fight.

"Don't think so, prick," said the large man in accented English as he walked menacingly toward Simon. The shorter man all but slithered toward Mai.

"Back off, asshole!" Simon barked as he instinctively reached into his shoulder holster for the Jericho – only to remember that it was sitting disassembled on the table, beside the armband. *Ah, fuck,* he thought.

The giant took another step closer and looked down at Simon with a cruel sneer. "Or what?" he asked confidently.

When the door had exploded open, Mai had sat down in shock on the couch. Simon quickly glanced over at her; she was petrified. Rat-face stood close, much too close, leering down at her.

Simon punched the giant across his face with his right hand as hard as he could. Unfazed, the man called to his companion as he maintained his gaze on Simon. "Hey Vu, the boss only wants the woman, right?" he asked. "I can kill this one?"

"Yeah, Pham," the rat-man responded, staring at Mai lustfully. "He didn't say we couldn't have a little fun of our own first, though."

Mai shuddered. Vu's carved smile was bad enough, but the hunger in his eyes was worse.

"You go first while I take care of this one," said Pham smugly. He cracked his knuckles in anticipation, and then his neck.

Vu grabbed Mai and began to tear at her shirt as she struggled to get free.

"I told you, back off!" barked Simon, only to be hit in the face with Pham's mighty blow. Simon stumbled backward and fell on his back, dazed.

Pham picked Simon up as effortlessly as one might pick up a cat. Holding Simon's shirt collar, Pham threw him across the room. Simon collided with the wall before falling to the floor.

Meanwhile, Mai was desperate to get Vu off of her. His odor was as vile as his intentions. She managed to break her hands free and scratched both cheeks with her nails. Recoiling in pain, Vu stood up, then yanked Mai off the couch and slapped her in the face. "Oh, I *like* it when they fight," Vu snarled, grabbing her with his other hand in a pincer grip.

On the other side of the room, Pham casually walked over to Simon as he picked himself up off the floor.

"C'mon, little man. Fight!" encouraged Pham.

Simon glanced over to Mai, his heart sinking at the sight of her struggling with Vu. *Gotta help her*, he thought.

Pham just stood there, smiling with condescension. Simon shot up from the ground and uppercutted Pham with his fist as hard as he could, then followed with right and left jabs to the face in quick succession. Simon smiled with satisfaction as the giant stumbled backward. He shot a glance at Mai, but before he could move towards her, Pham recovered with a backhand that sent Simon reeling.

Vu grabbed Mai by her shirt, pulling her towards him. She willed herself not to faint, but her head was spinning in shock.

Pham punched Simon in the stomach and then with his other arm grabbed Simon's neck and lifted him up. Simon struggled to free himself from Pham's grip even as Pham started to squeeze. Out of the corner of his eye he saw that Vu had forced Mai back onto the couch, holding her down on her stomach with pressure on the back of her neck with one hand, as he pulled off her jeans with the other. Mai's screams of fear and protest were heartbreaking. Vu held her down with one foot as he unzipped his fly.

"Hey Vu, hurry up!" Pham yelled to his companion.

Simon continued to gasp for air under Pham's grip but he'd heard the zipper, too. Desperate to get free, Simon began punching Pham in his nose as hard as he could.

Suddenly there was the crack of broken glass. A red hole appeared in Pham's forehead. He fell to the floor, blood spurting from the wound, taking Simon down with him.

The sound of bodies falling to the floor distracted Vu. He snapped his head up, utterly surprised to see Pham's body on the floor in a growing pool of blood. Simon appeared to be dead as well.

Vu shrugged and turned his attention back to Mai. *More time for me*, he muttered.

Simon lay on top of Pham's lifeless body, weak and bruised from the exhausting fight. Mai's cries for help seemed to come from far away. "Simon!" she screamed. Vu's violation of her was imminent.

Instantly, Simon's head cleared. He reached for the revolver in his ankle holster. *Should have used this the second these bastards showed up,* he thought as he rose and pulled back the pistol's hammer. He aimed the pistol at the back of Vu's neck and fired. Blood shot from Vu's neck and onto Mai as she pushed his body off of her and onto the floor dead.

Simon had needed one rush of adrenaline to get the job done, but now he was spent. With dwindling reserves of strength he stood up, still with the forethought to grab his trench coat before stumbling towards Mai.

Mai lay silent, her body quivering in shock, her face still contorted in abject horror. Her head, shirt, underwear and naked legs were covered in Vu's blood. Her jeans were crumpled around her ankles, but her underwear was still on. *Thank God,* Simon thought.

As Simon neared the couch, Mai started crying uncontrollably. She rolled off onto the floor leaning against the couch. Bringing her knees up to her face, she wrapped her arms around her legs and buried her head as she shook with great sobs. Simon laid his coat around her and sat on the couch, stroking her hair.

Gently he leaned down and put his arms around her to comfort and reassure her. "Shh, shh. It's over."

As soon as Mai felt Simon's embrace, her shaking stopped. She looked up at him, her face covered in Vu's blood mixed with her own tears.

Simon's face was bloodied and bruised as well. "It's okay, just let it out Mai," Simon said softly. Mai buried her head in his arms as she continued to cry.

As Mai wept, Simon looked up at the window. There was a bullet hole – obviously made by the bullet that killed Pham, but whose bullet was it? *Fuck it.* He slipped onto the floor beside Mai and held her, leaning against the couch. They were both damaged, although in different ways, but they stayed like that, side by side, leaning on one another, until they both fell asleep as the horrible predawn melted into a better morning.

*****

On the roof of a building across the street from the room where Simon and Mai slept, Kenji Yamada reloaded his SR-25 sniper rifle. He briefly wondered who was responsible for the second gunshot in the apartment. What really concerned him was who was on the *receiving* end of the shot. If it was Simon, then that would not only cost them money but complicate things with Silhouette.

He was unsure who the girl was, but he knew it was now a major priority to make sure that both of them got to the *Zheng* intact. Otherwise, at the very least, he and Flying Fish wouldn't get paid. *There's no point in worrying about it, I'll know the score soon enough,* he thought.

Chapter 20

Hog Outta Hell

Simon Kane and Mai Yunao awoke close to noon, still on the floor in front of the couch.

"You okay?" Simon asked as the sun's rays shone through the cracked glass window into the room.

Mai nodded as she wiped the sleep from her eyes.

Simon stood up slowly. Since the fight with Pham, his chest, back and body still ached, but he tried not to let it show. He walked over to the table to reassemble the Jericho.

As Mai lowered her hands, she saw that they were covered in dried blood. Looking up, she saw the dead bodies of Vu and Pham and flinched, at the horrid memory of last night.

That was no dream; it was a living, waking nightmare. She noticed something shining on the floor on the other side of the room, and crawled over to it, not even noticing that her jeans were still wrapped around her ankles.

In a daze, she picked up the object. It was the little revolver Simon had used to kill Vu. The memory of the attack rushed back and she began to shake again as tears welled up in her eyes. She dropped the pistol and tightened her grip on Simon's trench coat around her.

As Simon holstered the reassembled Jericho, he heard the pistol fall. Turning, he saw that Mai was crying again. He gently helped her up.

"Mai, it's okay. Shhh. He's gone now; he can't hurt you," Simon said soothingly.

At his touch, Mai stopped shaking as she had done last night. The daze cleared, and she turned to embrace Simon tightly. She almost knocked the still-weak Simon off balance, but he caught himself – and did the only think he could think of. He embraced her in return, their breaths synchronizing as they held each other. After a full minute, Mai loosened her grip and looked up at Simon, wiping the tears from her face, smearing Vu's blood as she did.

"I'm sorry I ruined your coat," said Mai with a weak smile, her composure returned as she let it fall to the floor.

"Don't worry; it's seen worse," said Simon with a sly grin.

She laughed, suddenly embarrassed. She quickly pulled her jeans up.

"I can't go out looking like this. Is there a shower in here or something?" asked Mai.

"There's a tiny one in the bathroom, but don't take too long," said Simon as he put the little pistol back in his ankle holster. "We need to get out of here."

"Okay," Mai said weakly as she closed the bathroom door behind her.

Simon tossed the trench coat on the table and put the wrist blade back onto his left hand. *Better check our location on the phone,* he thought. He heard the water turn on and smiled a little.

The tiled enclosure was small and dingy, but Mai barely noticed as she disrobed and turned the knob on the wall. Beneath the steaming spray, she harshly rubbed her face, her arms, anywhere the vile man had touched her, letting the water wash away all traces of him.

While Mai showered, Simon sat down to check the GPS. He was both surprised and relieved to discover how near they were to the *Zheng*. "Almost there," Simon muttered aloud.

A few minutes later, Mai exited the shower and got dressed. "Well?" she asked as she came out, a cloud of steam coming with her.

Simon did not comment. Her face and hands were clean, but the clothes she had put back on were still stained with last night's terror. Her shirt was torn, but not enough to be immodest. It would have to do for now.

"We aren't that far from the *Zheng*," Simon explained as he put the phone back into his pocket. "If we leave now we should be there in an hour and a half, assuming there are no more surprises."

"No surprises would be nice," grunted Mai, sounding better.

"Then let's get the hell out of here," Simon replied as he stood up to put his trench coat on.

"Fine by me," said Mai, eager to leave the building and its memories behind.

Simon walked into the hallway to make sure it was safe. As Mai followed, she glanced back at the bodies. At the last minute, she spat on Vu before joining Simon in the stairwell.

"Who do you think fired that bullet through the window last night?" asked Mai as they walked down the stairs.

"Dunno," Simon said with a shrug; he wondered the same thing. First, the help in the alley after the chopper pilot had given his life to save then, and now this. They had a guardian angel, but who? Or was that angel actually a devil in disguise?

"With the truck broken down, how will we get to the ship?" asked Mai as they walked down the stairs. She was unclear about Simon's time calculations. *An hour and a half walking? Biking? What?*

"Those assholes from last night must have gotten here in something," Simon answered as he opened the front door and walked outside. "We might not have to walk after all."

As they exited the building they were greeted with a gust of cool Pacific air. The near constant explosions and gunfire of the previous day had diminished considerably. What they still heard, though fairly constant, seemed to come from a further distance.

Simon's gaze swept the street as he ventured away a bit. To his surprise, two motorcycles were behind the useless truck. Simon called Mai over.

"Motorcycles? You must be joking," Mai grunted, as if in disapproval.

"What's the problem?" asked Simon as he began to hot-wire one of them.

"I don't know how to drive a motorcycle," Mai protested.

"Fortunately, I do," said Simon as the engine started with a loud throbbing rumble. He got on the bike, grabbed the handle bars and revved the engine with a satisfied grin, gesturing with his head for her to get on behind him.

"Americans," muttered Mai as climbed onto the seat behind Simon, wrapping her arms tightly around his chest. Simon released the brake and eased around the truck in front of them.

"Hold on!" Simon called back to her. "Here comes the fun part!" Simon twisted the throttle and the bike shot forward like the proverbial bat out of hell.

Simon could tell Mai was not enjoying the ride, as her arms had his torso in a vise grip. Suddenly they heard what sounded like a truck behind them. Simon and Mai both turned around; a Cartel gun truck was gaining on them fast.

"Simon! Behind us!" Mai yelled.

"I know!" barked Simon.

Unknown to Simon and Mai, however, Kenji Yamada was behind the truck on his motorcycle. He pulled out the China Lake with one hand and fired a grenade at the truck, destroying it in a fiery explosion. Kenji, his other hand still on the throttle, swerved the bike out of the way of the smoldering Cartel truck.

Mai and Simon looked behind at the explosion, hoping to see who or what had caused it. The figure of a man on a motorcycle grew smaller as he sped farther and farther away.

"Who the hell is that?" Mai yelled.

"Good question," replied Simon as he made a left at an intersection.

They zigzagged down several streets as Kenji backtracked and followed them at a discreet distance. After a while, with no further delays, Mai relaxed enough to appreciate the ride. As they arrived at the docks, they both smiled; soon they would be safe.

The docks were filled with large rectangular shipping crates and a few buildings scattered here and there. After a few minutes of weaving through the maze that was Sankan harbor they spotted the *Zheng*.

"That's it! It must be," said Simon over his shoulder, his voice filled with relief.

Just as victory seemed to be within their grasp, the staccato sound of gunfire erupted behind them. The bike suddenly swerved uncontrollably.

"Fuck! Something hit the wheel!" Simon yelled as he struggled to maintain control.

"Two Cartel trucks coming!" barked Mai as she again tightened her grip on Simon.

"We either jump off or crash!" yelled Simon.

"What?" Mai cried.

"Cover your head first!" barked Simon. "*Now!*"

They jumped off the bike, rolling on the ground as the bike crashed into a shipping container. Simon stood, ignoring the shooting pain through his entire body. He helped Mai get up. "Are you okay?" he asked.

"Yes," Mai answered weakly. "I think so."

The trucks had stopped behind them; the Cartel commandos resumed the barrage of gunfire. As Simon and Mai ran for cover behind a shipping container, Simon felt a sudden sharp pain in his right shoulder. Instinctively he placed his left hand on his shoulder, doing his best to ignore the all-too-familiar pain of a gunshot. Warm blood poured down his arm.

They hid behind the metal shipping container as the gunmen slowly advanced.

"Oh my God, you've been shot!" exclaimed Mai in a loud whisper. "Let me help you!" She had no idea *how*, but maybe there was something...

"Don't worry about it, kid. I'm not dying here and neither are you," said Simon defiantly. "But hand me my gun." Mai reached under the trench coat and unholstered the Jericho for him.

His right arm all but useless from pain, Simon took the Jericho with his left and leaned out from cover. He fired several shots at the approaching gunmen. After killing two of them, he leaned back behind cover. As he reloaded the pistol clumsily and painfully, he was suddenly dizzy. He collapsed on the ground beside a puddle of his own blood.

"Simon wake up! You've lost too much blood!" yelled Mai.

Simon drifted momentarily out of consciousness, and then back. Lightheaded, his perception of his surroundings began to blur. What looked like a missile flew overhead, followed by an explosion. Then a salvo of automatic gunfire, the pounding of boots on the ground, screaming in Mandarin and Portuguese.

He could just make out a figure walking towards him with a gun. *A woman?* Before his mind could even formulate the question – *Who is that?* – the world went black, cold and silent.

Chapter 21

Down Too Long in the Midnight Sea

When the darkness and silence receded, Simon – alive, much to his surprise – awoke. He was lying in what looked like a hospital room, but the slight listing back and forth told him he was on a ship. When he tried to stand up, he couldn't move his hands or his legs. He took a visual inventory as best he could: hospital gown, wrists and ankles strapped to the bed, a medical bandage on his forehead that had slipped annoyingly close to his good eye. There was a door in front of the bed and a bathroom on the far left of the room.

There were two chairs. One next to his bed, the other was on the far side of the room – which, in the close quarters, was none too far. Next to that chair was a cabinet, its doors open to reveal his clothes hanging inside. *I hope somebody sent the coat out to be dry-cleaned*, he thought wryly. A tray table nearby held a scalpel, some bottles. On both sides of the bed was medical equipment, and a heart monitor.

Simon's mind raced with questions, primarily *Where am I?* and *Where is Mai? As* he studied the ceiling for answers, the door opened. Deng walked in wearing his trademark black trench coat, pants and tie, with white dress shirt and tea shade sunglasses. *He always looks like he just stepped out of a John Woo movie,* Simon thought.

Deng locked the door behind him, a smirk on his face when he gazed down at Simon.

"We aren't done with you yet," said Deng, grinning.

"Guess I'll have to try harder," grunted Simon sarcastically.

"If you must," replied Deng equally sarcastic.

Simon strained his wrists against the restraints. "Is there a reason for the restraints?" Simon asked.

"Security and safety. We couldn't have you running around the ship in your condition," said Deng, removing the straps before sitting down on the chair next to the bed. "You'd lost a lot of blood. We weren't sure how it might affect you, once you woke up."

"Fair enough. I was really out of if it. Where are we?" inquired Simon, adjusting the bandage so he could see better. It felt great to be able to move.

"En route to Taiwan aboard the *Zheng*," explained Deng. "I must say I'm surprised you and Mai are alive at all, considering the beating you took from the Smiling Boys, the shootout, the bike crash and getting shot at the harbor," Deng continued. "But the doctor says you're fine now. You'll be able to take it easy for the duration of the trip, anyway."

"I aim to please," muttered Simon dryly.

Deng had not, however, mentioned Mai. "What about Mai? Is *she* okay?" Simon asked anxiously.

"Don't worry about her, either," Deng nodded. "She is fine as well, just a few scratches and bruises. Though from what she told us it could have been a hell of a lot worse had it not been for your skills and care. She surely would have been raped ... killed, no doubt, if you hadn't killed the bastards when you did," he said gratefully.

Simon relaxed somewhat, relieved Mai was okay. Evidently she had not mentioned their guardian angel, either. *Probably wise.* "What about our deal?" he asked.

Deng removed his sunglasses. "Once we get to Taiwan, you, me and Mai will board a plane to Hong Kong where the Mountain Master will discuss further aspects of the deal with the two of us," Deng explained, gesturing back and forth. Apparently Mai would not be part of that discussion. *As she would prefer, I'm sure,* thought Simon.

There was a loud knocking on the door. "Ah, that should be Mai now," said Deng as he put his sunglasses back on. He unlocked the door, opening it.

Mai rushed into the room and over to Simon, embracing him tightly. "Simon! You're awake!" she said, overjoyed.

The embrace was painful, but Simon was glad to see her looking so well. As she stood up, he smiled at her. The force of her hug had left her glasses askew, which she quickly fixed.

"You clean up pretty well," he said. Her bloody clothes were replaced by a white dress shirt and black jeans.

"I'm surprised by the visit, but pleased," Simon said.

"She's been by your side practically the whole time," Deng explained. "We had to pry her away from you so the ship's doctor could operate. Only when she knew you were going to be alright did she let them tend to her, too."

Mai could not help herself. She leaned down to hug him again. "Mai. I appreciate the hug but it's too...," started Simon, wincing in pain.

"Oh, I'm sorry." Mai was embarrassed as she let go.

"Don't be sorry," Simon waved to her weakly, but with a sly grin. "It's not every day I get hugged by a beautiful woman."

Mai blushed as she sat down, unconsciously scooting the chair a little closer.

Deng backed toward the door. "I think I'll be going – let you two catch up," he said. He wasn't sure how he felt about the chemistry in the room. Then again, they had been through a lot. Perhaps that was all it was.

Deng planned to go to the office he maintained on board the *Zheng*, but as he closed the door to Simon's room behind him, he heard a voice from the shadows and turned.

"How is he today?" queried the voice.

Sasha Molotova leaned against the wall next to the door to Simon's room. Her arms were crossed in front of her.

"He's fine, Molotova," Deng answered.

"Good," replied Sasha, not changing her expression. Inwardly, the news elated her.

"I know you two have a history," said Deng.

"You could say that," Sasha answered.

"Is that why our security cameras spotted you leaving Simon's room the other night? Because of *history*?" Deng asked, his eyebrows raised as he stepped closer to her.

"Must have been a bird," Sasha replied dismissively.

"Birds don't use grappling guns," said Deng, inching closer.

"Only the birds that can't fly," replied Sasha dryly. She had not shifted her weight even slightly at his advance.

Deng decided not to press the issue further. He turned with a shrug, and continued to his office. Only then did Sasha settle into a more relaxed stance, resuming her post by Simon's room. *Certainly is quiet in there,* she thought.

On the other side of the wall, Simon and Mai were silently assessing one another. Mai seemed to be uninjured, Simon observed, but he wondered about the kind of trauma that might lurk within.

"I think we could use some air," Mai noted as she got up to open the porthole.

"Sheila," said Simon.

"What?" asked Mai as she managed the latch, confused.

"You asked me what the name of the woman I lost was, the person I'm trying to avenge. Her name was Sheila Goodbody," said Simon.

"Wait … the writer?" asked Mai, frowning.

"Yeah," Simon answered.

"That was her real name? Not a pseudonym?" Mai inquired. "I always thought she was just being cute."

Simon chuckled at her remark, which hurt a bit, a reminder of Pham's brutal blows and the harbor attack not that long ago. A more pleasant reminder was the image of meeting Sheila for the first time. He'd teased her about her name. "I'm serious," said Simon.

Mai stood at the porthole and let the brisk ocean breeze sweep over her face for a few seconds. Simon watched her hair move a little as she stood there with her eyes closed.

"Have you changed your mind at all about seeking revenge for her death?" asked Mai.

"Hell no. And don't even try to convince me otherwise," said Simon stubbornly.

"I wouldn't think of it," Mai said as she sat again. "But I'm curious. If your roles were reversed and you had been killed instead. What do you think she would do?" asked Mai.

"The exact damn thing I'm doing. Without hesitation," Simon answered. "Don't you think I've asked myself that same question?"

Mai was a little taken aback at the suddenness and strength of his answer. "You must have really loved each other," Mai replied.

Simon smiled sadly. "I always wondered what she saw in a bum like me," he said.

"Yeah, I don't see it either," quipped Mai.

"That sense of humor of yours – you sure keep it hidden most of the time," said Simon sarcastically.

Mai smiled, realizing she wouldn't get anywhere arguing with him. She decided to change the subject.

"There is a strikingly beautiful Russian woman with an eye patch out in the hallway. Do you know her?" Mai inquired.

So she is *here,* thought Simon. "What about her?" he replied, his tone even.

"I'm just curious. Do you know her?" Mai asked.

"You might say that. She and I had some ... laughs ... a long time ago," answered Simon.

"Who is she?" asked Mai.

"A former spy for Russia. Now she's an international mercenary," Simon answered. "Why the curiosity?"

Mai shrugged a little. "After you were shot, and the Triad came to rescue us from the Cartel, she was with them. She paid particular attention to you," Mai explained, adding, "that's all."

"I'm touched," said Simon disingenuously. No way did he want to get into his relationship with Sasha right now. "Anyway, how're you holding up, kid?" he asked Mai.

When Mai shivered a little, Simon instantly regretted bringing it up. *That was just hours ago, moron. Of course she's still feeling it.*

Mai recovered quickly, though, and put on a brave face. "Fine, just fine. A few cuts from the bike crash, but other than that I'm ... fine." She rolled her eyes. "I already said that, didn't I?" She shook her head a little and looked across the room, not making eye contact. "The doctor says that I might need therapy because of the ... what happened," she said.

"You gonna go? To therapy, I mean?" Simon asked.

Mai was earnest as she met his gaze. "Of course! You should go too. It might help you cope with your loss," she said.

"Don't need it, but thanks anyway," Simon replied.

Mai stood up. "I'm sorry. I have to go, but ... just think about what I said," she said as she walked to the door. Mai closed the door behind her. Outside the room she punched the corridor wall. "Dammit!" she hissed.

"You'll hurt your hand if you keep that up," said Sasha wryly, stepping out of the shadows.

Mai whipped around in frustration. "What the hell is wrong with you people?" she barked.

"I wouldn't expect you to understand," Sasha replied quietly.

"Seriously, how can you people function in this endless loop of murder and revenge?! It burns you up from inside and leaves you with … nothing," Mai cried.

"On the contrary," Sasha said, shaking her head. "That's what keeps you warm inside when the world is cold."

The two women just looked at each other. Mai saw the determination in Sasha's eyes; Sasha was a little surprised at what she read in Mai's.

"I give up," Mai grunted as she turned and walked down the hall.

Sasha studied the doorknob of Simon's room, wondering if she should go inside and speak with him. There were good reasons not to … she shook her head to dismiss them, and opened the door. As she walked in, Simon smiled slightly.

"I got your note," said Simon.

"You're even harder to kill than I thought," said Sasha smugly.

Simon smirked. "You would know," he retorted.

"I suppose so," Sasha said dismissively, bouncing a little on her tiptoes.

"So what are you doing here? I thought you worked for the Vasilev Syndicate," Simon asked.

Sasha sat down in the chair next to the bed. "I work for whoever is paying. When I completed my mission for the Syndicate, the Guild notified me that the Triad wanted extra security on the way to Taiwan, so … I took the job," explained Sasha with a little shrug. Both of them knew that she had other reasons than money for taking it.

"Why would they need to hire outside security? Doesn't the Triad have enough people?" Simon asked.

"More than enough," Sasha said dryly. "But they're busy dealing with the remains of the Rojas Cartel. Besides ... we believe the Cartel might try to attack the ship on the way to Taiwan. A last ditch effort," she continued.

"Speaking of which, what's the story with the Cartel and Sankan?" asked Simon.

"Shortly after we left, the Cartel's leader apparently contacted the head of the Syndicate's Pakhan and the Triad's Mountain Master. They began negotiating terms of surrender," Sasha explained. "Seal the deal, then come after us anyway, maybe." She held up a hand, as if to stop the shop talk. "How are you doing, Simon?" she asked.

"Fine." *There's the word of the day*, he thought. "It's not like I haven't been shot before," said Simon dismissively.

"Ah yes; how could I forget Tripoli?" Sasha asked, leaning back in the chair and crossing her impressively long legs.

"Good question. Especially since you pulled the trigger," said Simon dryly.

"Details, details," said Sasha. It felt good to get back to the old banter.

"So where's your next job?" Simon asked. "After Taiwan?"

"I won't be taking any jobs for a while," Sasha said, crossing her arms for emphasis.

"Oh? Did you suddenly grow a conscience?" asked Simon sarcastically.

Sasha grinned. "Hardly," she said as she pulled one of the Aquarius discs out of a pouch in her red belt. "I have some scores to settle," Sasha said with an unsettling smile, waving the disc in the air.

Simon nodded. Whoever was going to be on the receiving end of that score had better get ready. "I know how you feel," said Simon as Sasha returned the disc to her pouch.

She stood to leave. "My offer still stands, Simon. After all, we 'one eyes' should stick together," Sasha said.

"Just like in Tauranga, right?" Simon asked dryly.

"Exactly," said Sasha as she opened the door. Smiling, she winked and blew a kiss coquettishly before closing the door behind her.

"Damn," muttered Simon, dismissing Sasha and the memory of their last night together. Just a few days ago ...

Still a little light-headed, Simon sat up to catch a glimpse of blue from the porthole Mai had opened. They were in open sea, of course, nothing but an endless expanse of blue, as if the sky and ocean had become one giant cerulean expanse that went on forever.

As he took a deep breath of the salt air, Dio's song "Holy Diver" came to mind for some reason. *You've been down too long ...*

He began to hum the tune as he lay his head back on the pillow. Eventually he fell into a deep, day-long sleep, his dream a mixture of faces: Sheila, Sasha.

Mai.

Chapter 22

Midnight in Waterfront City

His dreams forgotten, Simon woke the next morning feeling refreshed and revitalized. Never inclined to stay in bed once the sun was up, he unplugged himself from the machines and got out of the bed, glad to see that he had regained the strength in his legs. He yawned, stretched and removed the bandages that patch worked all over his body. In the bathroom mirror he saw that his black eye had all but disappeared. The hot water of the shower soothed his skin.

Walking naked to the cabinet, Simon was grateful to find that his clothes were cleaned, patched and pressed, including his trench coat. Someone had gone to a lot of trouble – even the bullet holes were sewn up. He dressed then checked both the revolver and the Jericho 941. No ammunition. His wrist blade was missing as well. Casually Simon slipped on his shoulder holster and placed the empty Jericho 941 in it; he did the same with the ankle holster and revolver. Even without ammunition, it just felt better having them close. The finishing touch was the trench coat.

After being confined for days, the idea of a walk around the ship was appealing. His legs needed a stretch, and it would give him the opportunity to discover where things were on board.

Outside the cabin door, he found himself in a long hallway with rooms on the left and right. Slipping his hands into his coat pockets, he began his expedition. A door at the end of the hallway led to an exterior deck with a solid railing on the port side. He stopped for a moment, breathing in the fresh salt air, gazing at the ocean and the sky. Judging by the sun's position, it was late afternoon. *Damn. Another day practically slept away. I must've needed it, though.* Simon headed for a flight of stairs that led to the ship's upper levels.

A woman's voice behind him yelled, "Pirates! Get down, asshole!"

Before he could react, the woman tackled him, bringing him down to the deck as a spray of machine gun bullets bounced off the side of the ship, narrowly missing them. As soon as the fusillade was over, the woman jumped to her feet, pulling two pistols out of dual shoulder holsters and aiming at an object off the opposite side of the deck. As Simon rose, he saw her target: a small boat off the starboard side. Surely they would be preparing to fire again.

Simon switched his gaze from the pirates to his surprise rescuer. She was a tall Hispanic woman in denim short-shorts, a white crop top, black finger-less gloves and combat boots. Her back was to him, but he could tell that the right side of her hair was shaved close with hair combed over to the left. *The fuck?* he thought.

"Who the hell are you?" Simon asked as she began shooting at the boat.

The woman barked over her shoulder at him as she fired. "The mother fuckin' tooth fairy. You armed?" she yelled.

"No," Simon replied, annoyed.

"Great! So fuckin' useless!" groused the woman as she continued firing at the pirates below.

When the pirates responded with another machine gun salvo, the woman ducked down beside Simon, shielded by the railing. He noticed a grenade hanging from her belt. Grabbing it, he pulled the pin and lobbed it with his uninjured arm at the boat. It landed in the middle of the gunmen and exploded, killing everyone. The boat immediately began to take on water.

"How's that for useless?" said Simon smugly as he stood up.

The woman holstered her pistols and angrily grabbed Simon by the collar of his trench coat with both hands.

"Listen, asshole, I *had* them. That was my last grenade!" the woman yelled as she pulled her right arm back to punch Simon.

Simon caught the punch with one hand before it connected, then quickly grabbed her by her neck with his other, swinging her around and pinning her against a nearby wall, so intent on the moment that he easily pushed through the pain.

Instead of giving in, she pressed a leg against the wall and pushed backwards with all of her strength, sending him backward and costing him his grip on her.

As they scrambled to their feet, the woman pulled out one of her pistols but Simon grabbed her wrist, squeezing it until she dropped her weapon. She reached for the other pistol, giving him time to swiftly pick up the other from the deck and take aim.

They faced each other silently, guns cocked, waiting for the other to shoot.

"Listen, lady. In the last week I have been kidnapped, hung by chains, chased, beaten and shot. Right now my patience is at its limit," he growled.

"So is mine, asshole," the woman retorted.

Someone unseen but nearby suddenly fired a gunshot into the air. "That's enough!" yelled the man authoritatively.

They turned at the sharp report of the blast. Standing a few yards away was a tall, muscular black man still holding up in the air what Simon recognized as a Desert Eagle pistol. Smoke wafted out of the barrel. *What the* – Simon thought. It was the man he had seen on the roof of the Triad's building in Sankan. Ben Martin, Deng had told him.

"Sorry, boss," said the woman with chagrin; she lowered her pistol.

These two must be more of Deng's mercenaries, thought Simon as he lowered the pistol.

"Forget about it," grunted Ben with a little wave, dismissing the incident as he walked towards them.

The woman held out her hand to Simon. "Yo, give it back," she said with impatience.

He handed the pistol to her as she held her glare. Holstering it, she never took her eyes off of him.

The man, however, extended a hand with a friendly smile. "Nice to finally meet you, Mr. Kane. 'Name's Ben," he said.

Simon shook the outstretched hand. "Let me guess. And offer my condolences," Simon said good-naturedly. "She's with you, right?" He glanced at the woman. She leaned against the railing with her arms crossed. *If looks could kill …,* he thought.

"Yeah," Ben said with a roll of his eyes. "I see you've already met, this is Fiona. We're part of the Flying Fish Trading Company," he explained.

"Deng told me about you guys, though he said there were three of you," Simon said.

"Kenji. He's on the other side of the ship," answered Ben, nodding his head in Kenji's direction.

"You're all ex-military?" Simon recalled from Deng's explanation.

"Damn right. Two of us are ex-Marine Force Recon," said Ben.

Simon grinned. Ben reminded him of a friend from Silhouette who'd also been in FORECON. "And this one?" Simon asked, gesturing to Fiona.

"None of your damn business," grunted Fiona smugly.

"What about you?" asked Ben, even though he already knew the answer, having read the files Connors sent him. He was curious as to the amount of information Simon might offer, however.

"SEAL Team 6," answered Simon.

"Are we supposed to be impressed?" asked Fiona.

"Depends. You know what they say about you FORECON guys," asked Simon with a knowing smirk.

"What?" Fiona asked.

"*Celer, Silens, Mortalis,*" Ben answered proudly.

Simon grinned upon hearing the motto of Marine Force Recon. Swift, Silent, Deadly. *An appropriate description of the last few days,* he thought.

"Why are you smiling, huh? Are we funny to you, asshole?" Fiona asked.

Simon kept the smile on his face. "No, I had a friend that was in FORECON," he explained.

"A friend, huh. Small world. Anyway, we should be going, Fiona," said Ben, turning.

Even couched in pleasant tones, Fiona knew an order when she heard one. She followed Ben up the stairs without looking back at Simon.

Simon shifted his gaze to the sea. The pirate ship had disappeared beneath the waves. It was as if it never existed.

*****

Several hours later at midnight in Kaohsiung City, Taiwan, the docks were quiet and empty. *This would make a good place for a murder,* thought Simon as he surveyed the scene from the deck. Simon and Mai had been told to disembark as soon the gangplank dropped. Simon held her by the elbow as they descended with Deng, each wondering what would happen next.

At the bottom, three black SUVs waited. Their drivers, identical in black suits, stood ready to open doors for their passengers. Simon guessed that one car was for Sasha and another was for the Flying Fish group, but no one else had shown up yet.

"Where are the others?" Simon asked Deng as they descended the gangplank.

"Asleep, would be my guess. My orders are to take you to the airport immediately upon arrival, however," Deng answered.

"Where are we going? I'm half-asleep," interrupted Mai, yawning.

"Hong Kong. The Mountain Master wishes to see you both as soon as possible," answered Deng as they approached the cars.

The three of them got into the car at the front of the line. They drove for what felt like hours. It was only twelve kilometers to the airport, but they drove past it to an isolated airfield at the edge of the city. Mai dozed on the way, her head falling onto Simon's shoulder.

A small plane was fueled there, waiting for them. Simon and Mai took a seat behind Deng.

As they taxied to the little runway for takeoff, Deng turned around and said, "Get comfortable. It's an hour and a half flight."

Simon and Mai didn't hear him, however. The engine had lulled them to sleep as soon as they sat down.

Chapter 23

One Down, Two to Go

When the plane landed in Hong Kong, Deng woke Simon and Mai and led them to another black SUV. Simon and Mai had slept well on the flight, but as it still before sunrise, they were a little groggy as they walked to the car.

The car took them across the city to the harbor, parking near a huge, gleaming yacht. Simon whistled, surprised at its massive size. *Nothing like coming aboard something like this to wake you up,* Simon thought appreciatively. He noticed that armed guards patrolled the parking lot and gangplank.

One of the guards approached them as they got out of the vehicle. "Weapons please," said the guard, looking straight at Simon.

Obediently, Simon removed his two guns and the wrist blade. The armband and ammunition had been returned to him just before they arrived in Taiwan, and now they were gone again. Begrudgingly, he handed them to the guard, who nodded at Deng in silent approval. Simon and Mai followed Deng up to the yacht.

The yacht's interior was magnificent, matching the exterior in sheer opulence. Compared to the *Zheng*, it looked like the inside of a penthouse. "I guess crime pays after all," Simon whispered to Mai. When she did not respond, Simon guessed the reason: She'd been here before. This was Lin Yunao's yacht, of course. The Mountain Master. Her father.

As they walked, they heard music playing throughout the yacht. Simon recognized the song but couldn't quite place the name of it. "Are you familiar with this?" he asked Mai, gesturing to the speakers along the way.

"Beethoven's 9th Symphony in D minor," explained Mai. "Classical music is one of my father's passions." She muttered, "And crime."

"I knew it sounded familiar," Simon said quietly. "Personally, I prefer Springsteen."

"Who?" Mai asked, inquisitive.

"The Boss?" said Simon. "Obviously." Mai's face was blank. "Seriously?" Simon rolled his eyes, surprised that she had never heard of Bruce Springsteen. "What you don't know would fill a library," he looked down at her with a smile.

Deng stopped them in front of two large wooden doors, gesturing to two silk brocade chairs that sat on either side of the doors. "Wait here while I talk to him first," said Deng.

They nodded and obediently sat in the chairs as Deng opened the doors and disappeared inside, the doors closing behind him. The music stopped abruptly. Simon and Mai could hear voices, but couldn't understand what they were saying.

After a minute, Deng returned. "He'd like to see you first, ma'am," he said, holding out a hand to Mai.

Mai stood up and walked into the office alone, closing the door behind her. Deng leaned against it, communicating clearly that

Simon was not to enter, regardless of anything he might hear.

The door remained closed for some time. "I wonder what they're talking about in there," commented Simon. "I got the idea they weren't exactly close."

"Only they know the answer to that. Although odds are that some of it involves you," Deng answered. "You would do well not to offer chance opinions about the Mountain Master."

"Point taken. Talking about me, eh? I'm just a popular guy," said Simon dryly.

"Don't let it go to your head," Deng answered flatly.

Simon shook his head. "The last time I did that … *this* happened" said Simon as he pointed to the patch over his eye.

"That must be quite a story," replied Deng. "Perhaps you can share it someday."

"You have no idea," Simon said, his eyebrows raising.

Before either of them could speak another word Mai exited the office and sat back down in the vacant chair. "Well?" Simon asked, impatient. So much time had led up to the exact moment.

"He wants to see you," Mai said simply, pointing over her shoulder to the door. Simon could tell that she had been crying, but now her face was impassive.

"Lucky me," muttered Simon. The last time he had seen Lin, he had been strung up by a chain. Surely this encounter, though, would be more positive.

Simon stood with an air of nonchalance, then walked to the doors as Deng stepped aside. He opened the doors and closed them before acknowledging his host with a little bow.

Lin sat behind a huge desk staring at Simon over tented hands. He did not rise.

The office was spacious, with bookcases on the walls to the right and left. They were filled with books of all sizes and colors, some ancient by the look of them, some new. Behind the desk was a huge computer screen showing a bright political map of the world. In front of the desk were two elegant leather chairs.

"Have a seat," Lin offered, gesturing with a slight wave of a hand.

Simon sat down cautiously, not sure what to expect. His mission complete, would Lin thank him? Kill him? He wished he still had his weapons.

"I thought it would be best for us to not meet in a dilapidated warehouse this time," quipped Lin, clearly enjoying himself. He glanced up at the carved ceiling. "And no chains."

"I gotta admit, it's a big improvement," said Simon, casually leaning back in the chair.

Lin grinned a little more widely.

"Obviously, this boat isn't the Triad's main headquarters, which is where I thought we were heading. It must be yours," Simon observed.

"Astute as ever, Mr. Kane," said Lin. He knew that Simon was not one for small talk, and neither was he. "Let's get down to business then."

"By all means, let's," Simon replied.

Lin sighed deeply. "First things first. Thank you for rescuing my daughter. You have my deepest gratitude," he began sincerely. Briefly, the man seemed to transform from organized crime boss to loving father.

"Don't mention it," Simon replied. Lin's mood and demeanor had changed since last they met. He was softer, noticeably more relaxed.

"Which brings us to the matter of your payment," Lin began.

Simon's heart rate quickened slightly. *Finally. The key to finding the Networc,* he thought.

"While you have been running across Sankan, I ordered my lieutenants across the globe to make finding Intel on the Networc their top priority," said Lin.

"Regrettably, however, the only success we have had is that we now know that their leader is known only as Mr. Zero," the old man continued.

Simon's heart sank. "That's it?" said Simon, trying to mask his disappointment.

"Yes, but be realistic, Mr. Kane. This one bit of information is more than you have found in three months! It will take more time to uncover the true identity and location of the elusive Mr. Zero," Lin said.

Simon knew that Lin was right but he hated having come this far, at such great risk, for what *felt*, at least, like a relatively small reward.

"Fortunately, within six months we should have more Intel on them," said Lin. "I am confident we will."

Simon calmed his inner fury. Lin was not a man he wished to disrespect, much less confront.

"So. What happens now?" he asked evenly.

"During the six months while we continue to track the Networc down, you will act as my daughter's bodyguard while she travels the world on her charity missions," said Lin. "I will allow her to return to her work, but only if you accompany her. She is agreeable to this. Not that that was necessary."

"While you are guarding her we will be assembling that team I mentioned," Lin continued.

There's the other part of the deal, remembered Simon. "And if you find nothing during those six months?" he asked.

"I am confident that we will find them. If, however, we are unsuccessful, you will be free to leave, as promised," explained Lin.

Simon hoped that Shakespeare was right about that "honor among thieves" idea. He leaned forward. Now that he knew the plan, he wanted details. "Who do you have in mind for this team exactly?" Simon asked.

"I have secured the services of two elite specialists. I will not identify them yet, but rest assured – they will help you get the job done," answered Lin.

Simon sighed. "So I guess that's it?" he said, his hands on his knees.

"It appears so," replied Lin. "As much as I would enjoy spending more time with my daughter, the timing is not ... optimal." Both men stood up and shook hands in agreement. "The car at the dock will take you and Mai to an apartment I have arranged, where you will rest for a few days," Lin explained. "You have ... both ... been through a lot."

"Whatever you say," said Simon as he walked out the door, closing the door.

Mai was sitting quietly in the chair, but Deng was no longer there. Simon crossed his arms and rolled his eyes in front of her. "I would seem that I'm stuck with you for a little longer."

Mai beamed. One chapter ended another begun. Where would the story end?

*****

Ten minutes later, Deng sat in front of the Mountain Master's desk again.

"Deng, I want you to spearhead the recruitment of our team to assist Simon," said Lin.

Deng was surprised, wanting to return to his work on the island as soon as possible. The negotiations, the cleanup ... it would take many months, if not years. "Sir, what about Sankan?" he asked.

"Mazin can handle the repairs. I'll talk with the Russians about who gets the Cartel's territory, how to divvy it up," explained Lin, waving his hands at the seeming insignificance of such matters.

Deng was inwardly annoyed by his new task, but also enticed by the challenge. "Whom do you have in mind for this team?" he asked.

Lin pulled two folders out of desk on his drawer and handed them to Deng. On one was written MAGIC 44, while on the other were the words Devil Woman. "Give them whatever they want in return for their help," Lin ordered.

Deng leafed through the folders for a few minutes then looked up, a worried look on his face.

It was Lin's turn to be annoyed, but he had no issue revealing it. "Is there a problem?" he asked brusquely.

"Just one that I see, sir. We have worked with MAGIC 44 in the past," said Deng. "He will not be difficult to find since he is an active Guild member."

"True," Lin nodded, anticipating Deng's concern.

Deng chose his words carefully. "I have no wish to offend you, sir, or question your Intel, but I had heard … sir … that the Devil Woman was killed years ago," he said.

"Do you also remember that she was an expert at every martial art, firearm and explosive tactic known to man?" Lin asked, raising his eyebrows. "She was so dangerous that in addition to being dubbed the Devil Woman, she was targeted by both the SAS and MI6 for elimination," he continued.

"These facts are known to me, yes. What is your point, sir?" Deng asked.

"Someone like that does not die, not in the manner that was reported. I have a hunch that she is not dead. Rather," Lin said dramatically, "I believe that she simply wishes *not to be found.*"

Lin's hunches had a way of eventually becoming reality; he was, in fact, well known for this.

"How do you propose that I find her, then?" asked Deng.

"Use our sources in Interpol. I have a theory that they aren't one hundred percent convinced of her death either," said Lin.

Deng took a deep breath, thinking briefly of the island. "How long do I have to find and contact these people, sir?" he asked.

"Six months," Lin answered, as if it would be an easy task, with a generous time frame.

"I see," Deng muttered. *'Might as well ask me to bring heaven to earth,* he thought to himself.

When Lin stood up, Deng followed suit. Lin came around the desk to shake Deng's hand, and then they exchanged bows. "Good luck," said Lin, as he gestured to the door.

"Thank you, sir," replied Deng. Clutching the files in his hands, he left the Mountain Master's office.

Deng could see a car waiting for him at the dock as he emerged onto the deck. He turned to look out to sea before he stepped onto the gangplank. Somewhere out there … somewhere in the distance … were MAGIC 44 and the Devil Woman.

He hoped he could find them. His life, no doubt, depended on it.

*The race to find the Devil Woman begins in
Book Three of the Shadow World saga:*
Hell To Pay...

About the Author

Robert Fisher was born in Long Branch, New Jersey. While attending Indian River State College, he began writing as a hobby that quickly turned into a passion for storytelling. After graduating from college he sought to have his work published. He can be contacted on Facebook and Twitter at @ShadowWorld19. Edge of the Abyss is his second book. If you enjoyed it, get ready, because the best is yet to come.....

Official Website of Shadow World Series
shadowworld96180901.wordpress.com

Other Books by Robert Fisher

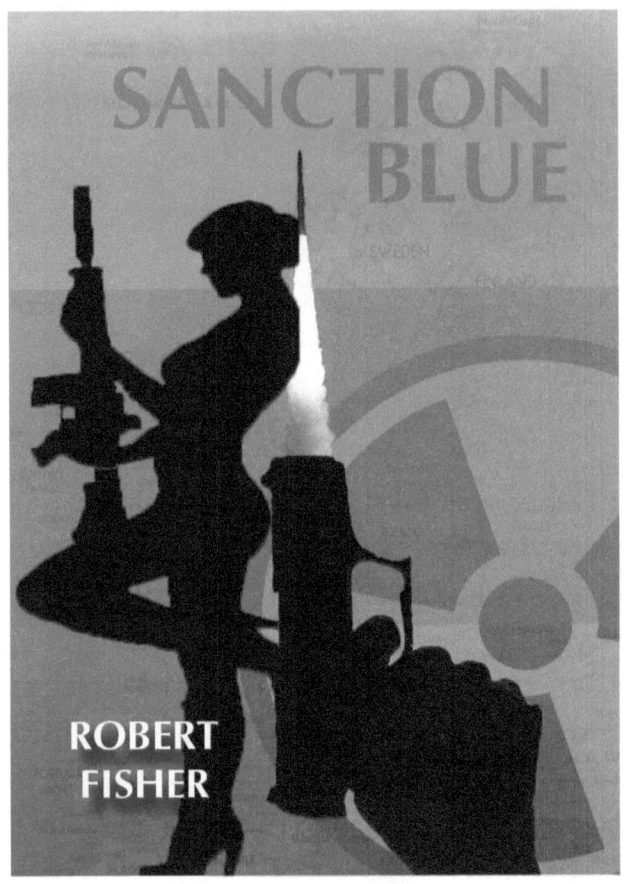